D1259829

THE FIRE EXTINGUISHERS DROPPED FROM THE *LUCIFER* INTO
THE FLAMES.

Tom Swift Among the Fire Fighters.   *Page* 200

TOM SWIFT AMONG THE FIRE FIGHTERS

OR

Battling with Flames from the Air

By

VICTOR APPLETON

AUTHOR OF "TOM SWIFT AND HIS MOTOR CYCLE," "TOM
SWIFT AND HIS AIR SCOUT," "TOM SWIFT AND HIS
UNDERSEA SEARCH," "THE MOVING PICTURE
BOYS SERIES," ETC.

ILLUSTRATED

NEW YORK
GROSSET & DUNLAP
PUBLISHERS

Made in the United States of America

BOOKS FOR BOYS
By VICTOR APPLETON
12mo. Cloth. Illustrated.

THE TOM SWIFT SERIES

THE MOVING PICTURE BOYS SERIES

GROSSET & DUNLAP, Publishers, New York

COPYRIGHT, 1921, BY
GROSSET & DUNLAP

Tom Swift Among the Fire Fighters

CONTENTS

iii

CONTENTS

TOM SWIFT AMONG THE FIRE FIGHTERS

CHAPTER I

A BAD PLACE FOR A FIRE

"IMPOSSIBLE, Ned! It can't be as much as that!"

"Well, you can prove the additions yourself, Tom, on one of the adding machines. I've been over 'em twice, and get the same result each time. There are the figures. They say figures don't lie, though it doesn't follow that the opposite is true, for those who do not stick closely to the truth do, sometimes, figure. But there you have it; your financial statement for the year," and Ned Newton, business manager for Tom Swift, the talented young inventor, shoved a mass of papers across the table to his friend and chum, as well as employer.

"It doesn't seem possible, Ned, that we have made as much as that this past year. And this, as I understand it, doesn't include what was taken from the wreck of the *Pandora?*"

Tom Swift looked questioningly at Ned Newton, who shook his head in answer.

"You really didn't get anything to speak of out of your undersea search, Tom," replied the young financial manager, "so I didn't include it. But there's enough without that."

"I should say so!" exclaimed Tom. "Whew!" he whistled, "I didn't think I was worth that much."

"Well, you've earned it, every cent, with the inventions of yourself and your father."

"And I might add that we wouldn't have half we earn if it wasn't for the shrewd way you look after us, Ned," said Tom, with a warm smile at his friend. "I appreciate the way you manage our affairs; for, though I have had some pretty good luck with my searchlight, wizard camera, war tank and other contraptions, I never would have been able to save any of the money they brought in if it hadn't been for you."

"Well, that's what I'm here for," remarked Ned modestly.

"I appreciate that," began Tom Swift. "And I want to say, Ned——"

But Tom did not say what he had started to. He broke off suddenly, and seemed to be listening to some sound outside the room of his home where he and his financial and business manager were going over the year's statement and accounting.

Ned, too, in spite of the fact that he had been busy going over figures, adding up long columns, checking statements, and giving the results to Tom, had been aware, in the last five minutes, of an ever-growing tumult in the street. At first it had been no more than the passage along the thoroughfare of an unusual number of pedestrians. Ned had accounted for it at first by the theory that some moving picture theater had finished the first performance and the people were hurrying home.

But after he had finished his financial labors and had handed Tom the first of a series of statements to look over, the young financial expert began to realize that there was no moving picture house near Tom's home. Consequently the passing throngs could not be accounted for in that way.

Yet the tumult of feet grew in the highway outside. Ned had begun to wonder if there had been an attempted burglary, a fight, or something like that, calling for police action, which had gathered an unusual throng that warm, spring evening.

And then had come Tom's interruption of himself when he broke off in the middle of a sentence to listen intently.

"What is it?" asked Ned.

"I thought I heard Rad or Koku moving around out there," murmured Tom. "It may be that my father is not feeling well and wants to speak to me or that some one may have telephoned. I told them not to disturb me while you and I were going over the accounts. But if it is something of importance——"

Again Tom paused, for distinctly now in addition to the ever-increasing sounds in the streets could be heard a shuffling and talking in the hall just outside the door.

"G'wan 'way from heah now!" cried the voice of a colored man.

"It *is* Rad!" exclaimed Tom, meaning thereby Eradicate Sampson, an aged but faithful colored servant. And then the voice of Rad, as he was most often called, went on with:

"G'wan 'way! I'll tell Massa Tom!"

"Me tell! Big thing! Best for big man tell!" broke in another voice; a deep, booming voice that could only proceed from a powerfully built man.

"Koku!" exclaimed Tom, with a half comical look at Ned. "He and Rad are at it again!"

Koku was a giant, literally, and he had attached himself to Tom when the latter had made one of many perilous trips. So eager were Eradicate and Koku to serve the young inventor that frequently there were more or less good-natured clashes between them to see who would have the honor.

The discussion and scuffle in the hall at length grew so insistent that Tom, fearing the aged colored man might accidentally be hurt by the giant Koku, opened the door. There stood the two, each endeavoring to push away the other that the victor might, it appeared, knock on the door. Of course Rad was no match for Koku, but the giant, mindful of his great strength, was not using all of it.

"Here! what does this mean?" cried Tom, rather more sternly than he really meant. He had to pretend to be stern at times with his old colored helper and the impulsive and powerful giant. "What are you cutting up for outside my door when I told you I must be quiet with Mr. Newton?"

"No can be quiet!" declared the giant. "Too much noise in street—big crowds—much big!"

He spoke an English of his own, did Koku.

"What are the crowds doing?" asked Ned. "I thought we'd been hearing an ever increasing tumult, Tom," he said to the young inventor.

"Big crowds—'um go to see big——"

"Heah! Let me tell Massa Tom!" pleaded Rad. Poor Rad! He was getting old and could not perform the services that once he had so readily and efficiently done. Now he was eager to help Tom in such small measure as carrying him a message. So it was with a feeling of sadness that Tom heard the old man say again, pleadingly:

"Let me tell him, Koku! I know all 'bout it! Let me tell Massa Tom whut it am, an'——"

"Well, go ahead and tell me!" burst out Tom, with a good-natured laugh. "Don't keep me in suspense. If there's anything going on——"

He did not finish the sentence. It was evident that something of moment was going on, for the crowds in the street were now running instead of walking, and voices could be heard calling back and forth such exclamations as:

"Where is it?"

"Must be a big one!"

"And with this wind it'll be worse!"

Tom glanced at Ned and then at the two servants.

"Has anything happened?" asked the young inventor.

"Dey's a big fire, Massa Tom!" exploded Rad.

"Heap big blaze!" added Koku.

At the same time, out in the street high and clear, the cry rang out:

"Fire! Fire!"

"Is it any of our buildings?" exclaimed Tom, in his excitement catching hold of the giant's arm.

"No, it's quite a way off, on de odder side of town," answered the colored man. "But we t'ought we'd better come an' tell yo', an'——"

"Yes! Yes! I'm glad you did, Rad. It was perfectly right for you to tell me! I wish you'd done it sooner, though! Come on, Ned! Let's go to the blaze! We can finish looking over the figures another time. Is my father all right, Rad?"

"Yes, suh, Massa Tom, he's done sleepin' good."

"Then don't disturb him. Mr. Newton and I will go to the fire. I'm glad it isn't here," and Tom looked from a side window out on many shops that were not a great distance from the house; shops where he and his father had perfected many inventions.

The buildings had grown up around the old Swift homestead, which, now that so much industry surrounded it, was not the most pleasant place to live in. Tom and his father only made this their stopping place in winter. In the summer they dwelt in a quiet cottage far removed from the scenes of their industry.

"We'll take the electric runabout, Ned," remarked Tom, as he caught up a hat from the rack, an example followed by his friend. Together the young inventor and the financial manager hurried out to the garage, where Tom soon had in operation a small electric automobile, that, more than once, had proved its claim to being the "speediest car on the road."

As they turned out of the driveway into the street they became aware of great crowds making their way toward a glow of sinister red light showing in the eastern sky.

"Some blaze!" exclaimed Tom, as he turned on more power.

"You said it!" ejaculated Ned. "Must be a general alarm," he added, as they caught the sound from the next street of additional apparatus hurrying to the fire.

"Well, I'm glad it isn't on our side of town," remarked Tom, as he looked back at the peaceful gloom surrounding and covering his own home and work buildings.

"Where do you reckon it is?" asked Ned, as they sped onward.

"Hard to say," remarked the young inventor,

as he steered to one side to pass a powerful imported automobile which, however, did not have the speed of the electric runabout. "A fire at night is always deceiving as to direction. But we can locate it when we get to the top of the hill."

Shopton, the suburb of the town where Tom lived, was named so because of the many shops that had been erected by the industry of the young inventor and his father. In fact the town was named Shopton though of late there had been an effort to change the name of the strictly residential section, which lay over the hill toward the river.

Tom's car shot up the slope with scarcely any slackening of speed, and, as he passed a group of men and boys running onward, Tom shouted:

"Where is it?"

"The fireworks factory!" was the answer.

"Fireworks factory!" cried Ned. "Bad place for a fire!"

"I should say so!" exclaimed Tom.

The chums had become gradually aware of the gale that was blowing, and, as they reached the summit of the hill and caught sight of the burning factory, they saw the flames being swept far out from it and toward a collection of houses on the other side of a vacant lot that separated the fireworks industrial plant from the dwellings.

As Tom Swift glimpsed the fire, noted its proportions and the fierceness of the flames, and saw which way the wind was blowing them, he turned on the power to the utmost.

"What are you doing, Tom?" yelled Ned.

"I'm going down there!" cried Tom. "That place is likely to explode any minute!"

"Then why go closer?" gasped Ned, for his breath was almost taken away by the speed of the car, and he had to hold his hat to keep it from blowing away. "Why don't you play safe?"

"Don't you understand?" shouted Tom in his chum's ear. "The wind is blowing the fire right toward those houses! Mary Nestor lives in one of them!"

"Oh—Mary Nestor!" exclaimed Ned. Then he understood—Mary and Tom were engaged to be married.

"They may be all right," Tom went on. "I can't be sure from this distance. Or they may be in danger. It's a bad fire and——"

His voice was blotted out in the roar of an explosion which seemed to hurl back the electric runabout and bring it to a momentary stop.

CHAPTER II

ONLY momentarily was Tom Swift halted in his progress toward the scene of the blaze in the fireworks factory. To him, and to the chum who sat beside him on the seat of the electric runabout, it appeared that the blast had actually stopped the progress of the car. But perhaps that was more their imagination than anything else, for the machine swept on down the hill, at the foot of which was the conflagration.

"That was a bad one, Ned!" gasped Tom, as he turned to one side to pass an engine on its way to the scene of excitement.

"I should say so! Must have been somebody hurt in that blow-up!"

"I only hope it wasn't Mary or her folks!" murmured Tom. "The wind is sweeping the fire right that way!"

"What are you going to do, Tom?" yelled his chum, as the business manager saw the young inventor heading directly for the blaze. "What's the idea?"

11

"To rescue Mary, if she's in danger!"

"I'm with you!" was Ned's quick response. "But you can't go any closer. The police are stretching the fire lines!"

"I guess they'll let me through!" said Tom grimly.

He slowed his car as he approached a place where an officer was driving back the throng that sought to come closer to the blaze.

"Git back! Git back, I tell you!" stormed the policeman, pushing against the packed bodies of men and boys. "There'll be another blow-up in a minute or two, and a lot more of you killed!"

"Are there any killed?" asked Tom, stopping the car near the officer.

"I guess so—yes. And some of the houses are catching. Git back now! You, too, with that car! You'll have to back up!"

"I've got to go through!" replied Tom, with tightening lips. "I've got to go through, Cassidy!" He knew the officer, and the latter now seemed, for the first time, to recognize the young inventor.

"Oh, it's you, is it, Mr. Swift?" he exclaimed. "Well, go ahead. But be careful. 'Tis dangerous there—very dangerous, an'——"

His voice was lost in the roar of another explosion, not as loud or severe as the first, but more plainly felt by Tom and Ned, for they were nearer to it.

"Now will you git back!" cried Policeman Cassidy, and the crowd did, without further urging.

Tom started the runabout forward again.

"We've got to rescue Mary!" he said to Ned, who nodded.

In another moment the two young men were lost to sight in a swirl of smoke that swept across the street. And while they are thus temporarily hidden may not this opportunity be taken of telling new readers something of the hero of this story?

The young inventor was introduced in the first volume of this series, called "Tom Swift and his Motor Cycle." It was Tom's first venture into the realms of invention, after he had purchased from Mr. Wakefield Damon a speedy machine that tried to climb a tree with that excitable gentleman.

Tom, with the help of his father, an inventor of note, rebuilt the motor cycle adding many improvements, and it served Tom in good stead more than once.

From then on the career of Tom Swift was steadily onward and upward. One new invention led to another from his second venture, a motor boat, through an airship and other marvels, and eventually to a submarine. In each of these vehicles of motion and travel Tom and his friends, Ned Newton and Mr. Damon, had many adventures, detailed in the respective volumes.

His venture in proceeding to save Mary Nestor from possible danger in the blaze of the fireworks factory was not the first time Tom had rendered service to the Nestor family. There was that occasion on which he had sent his wireless message from Earthquake Island, as related in an earlier volume.

Space forbids the detailing of all that had happened to the young inventor up to the time of the opening of this story. Sufficient to say that Tom's latest achievement had been the recovery of treasure from the depths of the ocean.

Tom Swift's activities in connection with his inventions had become so numerous that the Swift Construction Company, of which Ned Newton was financial manager and Mr. Damon one of the directors, had been formed. And when the rumor came that there was a chance to salvage some of the untold wealth at the bottom of the sea, Tom was interested, as were his friends.

It was decided to search for the wreck of the *Pandora,* sunk in the West Indies, and one of

Tom's latest submarine craft was utilized for this purpose.

Not to go into all the details, which are given in the last volume of this series, entitled "Tom Swift and His Undersea Search," suffice it to say that the venture was begun. Matters were complicated owing to the fact that Mary Nestor's uncle, Barton Keith, was in trouble over the loss of valuable papers proving his title to some oil lands. Mary mentioned that a person, Dixwell Hardley, was the man who, it was supposed, was trying to defraud her relative. And the complications may be imagined when it is said that this same Hardley was the man who had interested Tom in the undersea search for the riches of the *Pandora*.

Tom had been at home some time now, and it was while going over his accounts with Ned, and, incidentally, planning new activities, that the cry of fire broke in on them.

"Whew, Tom, some heat there!" gasped Ned, lowering his arm from his face, an action which had been necessitated by Tom's daring in driving the car close to the blazing fireworks factory.

"I should say so!" agreed Tom. "I can almost smell the rubber of my tires burning. But we're out of the worst of it."

"Lucky she didn't take the notion to blow up

as we were passing," grimly commented Ned. "Where are you aiming for now?"

"Mary's house. It's just beyond here. But we can't see it on account of the smoke."

A few seconds later they had passed through the black pall that was slashed here and there with red slivers of flame, and, coming to a more open space, Ned and Tom cleared their eyes of smoke.

"I guess there's no immediate danger," remarked Tom, as he saw that the home of Mary Nestor and the houses near her residence were, for the time being, out of the path of the flames. The explosion had blown down part of the blazing factory nearest the residential section, and the flames had less to feed on.

But the conflagration was still a fierce one. Not half the big factory was yet consumed, and every now and then there would sound dull, booming reports, causing nervous screams from the women who were out in front of their homes, while the men would crouch down as though fearing a shower of fiery embers.

"Oh, Tom, I'm so glad you're here!" cried Mary, as the runabout drew up in front of her home. "Do you think it will be much worse?" and she clutched his arm, as he got down to speak to her.

"I think the worst is over, as far as you people here are concerned," the young inventor replied. "The wind has shifted a bit."

"And there are several engines near us, Tom," said Mr. Nestor, coming forward. "The firemen tell me they will play streams of water on the roofs and outsides of our houses if the flames start this way again."

"That ought to do the trick," said Tom, with a show of confidence. "Anybody hurt around here?" he asked. "One of the policeman said he heard several were killed."

"They may have been—in the factory," said Mr. Nestor. "Of course if the fire and explosions had taken place in the daytime the loss of life would have been great. But most of the workers had left some time before the blaze was discovered. There are a few men on a night shift, though, and I shouldn't be surprised but what some of them had suffered."

"Too bad!" murmured the young inventor. "You're not worried about your home, are you, Mrs. Nestor?" he asked of Mary's mother.

"Oh, Tom, I certainly am!" she exclaimed. "I wanted to bring out our things, but Mr. Nestor said it wouldn't be of any use."

"Neither it would, if we've got to burn, but I don't believe we have—now," said her husband.

"That last explosion and the shift of the wind saved us. I appreciate your coming over, Tom," he went on. "We might have needed your help. It's queer there isn't some better, or more effective, way of fighting a fire than just pouring on a comparatively insignificant bit of water," he added, as, from what was now a safe distance, they watched the firemen using many lines of hose.

"They do have chemical extinguishers," said Ned.

"Yes, for little baby blazes that have just started," went on Mr. Nestor. "But in all the progress of science there has not been much advance in fighting fires. We still do as they did a hundred years ago—squirt water on it, and mighty little of it compared to the blaze. It would take a week to put this fire out by the water they are using if it were not for the fact that the blaze eats itself up and has nothing more to feed on."

"We'll have to get Tom to invent a new way of fighting fire," remarked Ned.

The young inventor was about to reply when several firemen, equipped with smoke helmets which they adjusted as they ran, came running down the street.

"What's the matter?" asked Tom of one whom he knew.

"Some men are trapped in a small shed back of the factory," was the answer. "We just heard of it, and we're going in after them. Oh! Oh—my—my heart!" he gasped, and he sank to the sidewalk. Evidently he was either overcome by the smoke and poisonous gases or by his exertions.

Tom grasped the situation instantly. Taking the smoke helmet from the exhausted fire-fighter, the young inventor shouted:

"I'll fill your place! See if you can grab a hat, Ned, and come on!"

One of the other firemen had two helmets, and he offered Ned one. Pausing only long enough to see that Mr. Nestor and some others were looking after the exhausted "smoke-eater," Ned raced on after Tom. The two young men, following the firemen, made their way around the end of the factory to the smoke-filled yard in the rear. But for the helmets, which were like the gas masks of the Great War, they would not have been able to live.

One of the firemen pointed through the luridly-lighted smoke to a small structure near the main building. This was beginning to burn. With quick blows of an axe the door was hewed down, and the rescue party, including Tom and Ned, made its way inside. In the light from the blaze, as it filtered through the windows, it could be seen that a man lay in a huddled heap on the floor.

By motions the leader of the rescue squad made it clear that the man was to be carried out, and Tom helped with this while Ned, using an axe, cleared away some débris to enable the door to be opened fully so the men could pass out carrying their burden.

The man was taken to the Nestor yard and stretched out on the grass. Word was relayed to one of the ambulance doctors who were on the scene attending to several injured firemen, and in a short time the man, who, it appeared, had been overcome by smoke, was revived.

"Well, that was a narrow squeak for you," said one of the firemen, glad to breathe without a mask on.

"Yes, it was touch and go," remarked the young doctor, who had used heroic measures to bring the man back from the brink of the grave. "But you'll live now, all right."

The revived man looked dully about him. He seemed somewhat bewildered.

"Of what use to live?" he murmured. "You might as well have let me die in there. Life isn't worth living now," and he sank into a stupor, while Tom and the others looked wonderingly at one another.

CHAPTER III

"WHAT'S the matter with him, Doctor?" asked Tom in a low voice of the young physician who had been working over the man. "Do you think he is worse hurt than appears? Is he dying, and is his mind wandering?"

"I don't believe so," answered the doctor. "At least I don't believe that he is dying, though his mind may be wandering. He isn't injured—at least not outwardly. Just temporarily overcome by smoke is what it looks like to me. But of course I haven't made a thorough examination."

"Hadn't we better get him into the house, Doctor?" asked Mr. Nestor, who stood with Tom, Ned and a group of men and boys about the inert form of the man lying on the grass. The rescued one was again seemingly unconscious.

"The best medicine he can have is fresh air," the doctor replied. "He's better off out here than in the house. Though if he doesn't revive presently I will send him to the hospital."

The man did not appear to be so badly off but what he could hear, and at these words he opened his eyes again.

"I don't want to go to the hospital," he murmured. "I'll be all right presently, and can go home, though—Oh, well, what's the use?" he asked wearily, as though he had given up some fight. "I've lost everything."

"Well, you've got a deal of life left in you yet; and that's more than you could say of some who have come out of smaller fires than this," said one of the firemen who, with Tom, had carried the man out of the shed. "Come on, we'd better be getting back," he said to his companion. "The worst of it is over, but there'll be plenty to do yet."

"You said it!" commented the other grimly.

They went out of the Nestor yard, many of the crowd that had gathered during the rescue following. The doctor administered some more stimulant in the shape of aromatic spirits of ammonia to the man, who, after his momentary revival, had again lapsed into a state of stupor.

"Who is he?" asked Tom, as the physician knelt down beside the silent form.

"I don't know," said Mr. Nestor. "I know quite a number connected with the fireworks factory, but this man is a stranger to me."

"I've seen him going into the main offices several times," remarked Mary, who was standing beside Tom. "He seemed to be one of the company officers."

"I don't believe so, Mary," stated her father. "I know most of the fireworks company officials, and I'm sure this man is not one of them. Poor fellow! He seems to be in a bad way."

"Mentally, as well as physically," put in Ned. "He acted as if sorry that we had saved his life."

"Too bad," murmured Mary, and then a policeman, who had just come into the yard to get the facts for his report, looked at the figure lying on the grass, and said:

"I know him."

"You do?" cried Tom. "Who is he?"

"Name's Baxter, Josephus Baxter. He's a chemist, and he works in the fireworks factory here. Not as one of the hands, but in the experiment laboratory. I've seen him there late at night lots of times. That's how I got acquainted with him. He was going in around two o'clock one morning, and I stopped him, thinking he was a thief. He proved his identity, and I've passed the time of day with him many a time since."

"Where does he live?" asked Mr. Nestor.

"Down on Clay Street," and the officer mentioned the number. "He lives all alone, so he told me. He's some sort of an inventor, I guess. At least I judged so by his talk. Do you want an ambulance, Doctor?" he asked the physician.

"No, I think he's coming around all right," was the answer. "If we had an auto we could send him home."

"I'll take him in the runabout," eagerly offered Tom. "But if he lives all alone will it be safe to leave him in his house?"

"He ought to be looked after, I suppose," the doctor stated. "He'll be all right in a day or so if no complications set in, but he'll be weak for a while and need attention."

"Then I'll take him home with me!" announced Tom. "We have plenty of room, and Mrs. Baggert will feel right at home with some one to nurse. Bring the runabout here, will you please, Ned?"

As Ned darted off to run up the machine, the man opened his eyes again. For a moment he did not seem to know where he was or what had happened. Then, as he saw the lurid light of the flames which were now dying away and realized his position, he sighed heavily and murmured:

"It's all over!"

"Oh, no, it isn't!" cheerfully exclaimed the doctor. "You will be all right in a few days."

"Myself, yes, maybe," said the man bitterly, and he managed to rise to his feet. "But what of my future? It is all gone! The work of years is lost."

"Burned in the fire?" asked Tom, wondering whether the man was a major stockholder in the company. "Didn't you have any insurance? Though I suppose you couldn't get much on a fireworks plant," he added, for he knew something of insurance matters in connection with his own business.

"Oh, it isn't the fire—that is directly," said the man, in the same bitter tones. "I've lost everything! The scoundrels stole them! And I—Oh, never mind!" he cried. "What's the use of talking? I'm down and out! I might just as well have died in the fire!"

Tom was about to make some remark, but the doctor motioned to him to refrain, and then Ned came up with the runabout. At first Josephus Baxter, which was the name of the man who had been rescued, made some objections to going to Tom's home. But when it was pointed out that he might lapse into a stupor again from the effects of the smoke poisons, in which event he would have no one to minister to him at his lonely home, he consented to go to the residence of the young inventor.

"Though if I do lapse into unconsciousness you might as well let me keep on sleeping until the end," said Mr. Baxter bitterly to Tom and Ned, as they drove away from the scene of the fire with him.

"Oh, you'll feel better in the morning," cheerfully declared Ned.

The man did not answer, and the two chums did not feel much like talking, for they were worn out and weary from their exertions at the fire. The factory had been pretty well consumed, though by strenuous labors the blaze had not extended to adjoining structures. The home of Mary Nestor was saved, and for this Tom Swift was thankful.

Mrs. Baggert, the Swift's housekeeper, was indeed glad to have some one to "fuss over," as Tom put it. She prepared a bed for Mr. Baxter, and in this the weary and ill man sank with a sigh of relief.

"Can I do anything for you?" asked Tom, as he was about to go out and close the door.

"No—thank you," was the halting reply. "I guess nothing can be done. Field and Melling have me where they want me now—down and out."

"Do you mean Amos Field and Jason Melling of the fireworks firm?" asked Tom, for the names were familiar to him in a business way.

"Yes, the—the scoundrels!" exclaimed Mr. Baxter, and from his voice Tom judged that he was growing stronger. "They pretended to be my friends, giving me a shop in which to work and experiment, and when the time came they took my secret formulæ. I believe that is what they started the fire for—to conceal their crime!"

"You don't mean that!" cried Tom. "Deliberately to start a fire in a factory where there was powder and other explosives! That would be a terrible crime!"

"Field and Melling are capable of just such crimes as that!" said Josephus Baxter, bitterly. "If they took my formulæ they wouldn't stop at arson."

"Were your formulæ for the manufacture of fireworks?" asked Tom.

"Not altogether," was the reply. "I had several formulæ for valuable chemical combinations. They could be used in fireworks, and that is why I could use the laboratory here. But the main use of my discoveries is in the dye industry. I would have been a millionaire soon, with the rise of the American dye industry following the shutting out of the Germans after the war. But now, with my secret formulæ gone, I am no better than a beggar!"

"Perhaps it will not be as bad as you think," said Tom, recognizing the fact that Mr. Baxter was in a nervous and excited state. "Matters may look brighter in the morning."

"I don't see how they can," was the grim answer. "However, I appreciate all that you have done for me. But I fear my case is hopeless."

"I'll see you again in the morning," Tom said, trying to infuse some cheerfulness into his voice.

He found Ned waiting for him when he came downstairs.

"How is he?" asked the young business manager.

"In rather a bad way—mentally, at least," and Tom told of the lost formulæ. "Do you know, Ned," he went on, "I have an idea!"

"You generally do have—lots of 'em!" Ned rejoined.

"But this is a new one," went on Tom. "You saw what trouble they had this evening to get a stream of water to the top stories of that factory, didn't you?"

"Yes, the pressure here isn't what it ought to be," Ned agreed. "And some of our engines are old-timers."

"Why is it necessary always to fight a fire with

water?" Tom continued. "There are plenty of chemicals that will put out a fire much quicker than water."

"Of course," Ned answered. "There are plenty of chemical fire extinguishers on the market, too, Tom. If your idea is to invent a new hand grenade, stay off it! A lot of money has been lost that way."

"I wasn't thinking of a hand grenade," said Tom, as he drew some sheets of paper across the table to him. "My idea is on a bigger scale. There's no reason, Ned, why a big fire in a tall building, like a sky-scraper, shouldn't be fought from above, as well as from below. Now if I had the right sort of chemicals I could——"

Tom paused in a listening attitude. There was the rush of feet and a voice cried:

"I'll get them! I'll get the scoundrels!"

CHAPTER IV

AN EXPERIMENT

"THAT can't be Koku and Rad in one of their periodic squabbles, can it?" asked Ned.

"No. It's probably Mr. Baxter," Tom answered. "The doctor said he might get violent once or twice, until the effects of his shock wore off. There is some quieting medicine I can give him. I'll run up."

"Guess I'd better go along," remarked Ned. "Sounds as if you'd need help."

And it did appear so, for again the frenzied shouts sounded:

"I'll get 'em! I'll get the scoundrels who stole my secret formulæ that I worked over so many years! Come back now! Don't put the match near the powder!"

Tom and Ned hurried to the room where the unfortunate chemist had been put to bed, to find him out in the hall, wrapped in a bedquilt, and with Mrs. Baggert vainly trying to quiet him. Mr. Baxter stared at Tom and Ned without seeing them, for he was in a delirium of fever.

"Have you my formulæ?" he asked. "I want them back!"

"You shall have them in the morning," replied Tom soothingly. "Lie down, and I'll bring them to you in the morning. And drink this," he added, holding out a glass of soothing mixture which the doctor had ordered in case the patient should become violent.

Josephus Baxter glared about with wild eyes, but between them Tom and Mrs. Baggert managed to get him to drink the mixture.

"Bah! It's as bad as some of my chemicals!" spluttered the chemist, as he handed back the glass. "You are sure you'll have my formulæ in the morning?" he asked, as he turned to go back to his room.

"I'll do my best," declared Tom cheerfully. "Now please lie down."

Which, after some urging, Mr. Baxter consented to do. Eradicate wanted to lie down in the hall outside the excited chemist's door to guard against his emerging again, but Tom decided on Koku. The giant, though not as intelligent as the colored man, was more efficient in an emergency because of his great strength. Eradicate was getting old, and there was a pathetic droop to his figure as he shuffled off when Koku superseded him.

"Ah done guess Ah ain't wanted much mo'," muttered Rad sadly.

"Oh, yes, you are!" cried Tom, as, the excitement over, he walked downstairs with Ned. "I'm going to start something new, Rad, and I'll need your help."

"Will yo', really, Massa Tom?" exclaimed faithful Rad, his face lighting up. "Dat's good! Is yo' goin' off after mo' diamonds, or up to de caves of ice?"

"Not quite that," answered the young inventor, recalling the stirring experiences that had fallen to him when on those voyages. "I'm going to work around home, Rad, and I'll need your help."

"Anyt'ing yo' wants, Massa Tom! Anyt'ing yo' wants!" offered the now delighted Rad, and he went to bed much happier.

"Well, to resume where we left off," began Ned, when he and Tom were once more by themselves, "what's the game?"

"Oh, I don't know that it's much of a game," was the answer. "But I just have an idea that a big fire in a towering building can be fought from above with chemicals, as well as from the ground with streams of water.

"Well, I guess it could be," Ned agreed. "But how are you going to get your chemicals in at the top? Shoot 'em up through a hose? If you do that you'll need a special kind of hose, for the chemicals will rot anything like rubber or canvas."

"I wasn't thinking of a hose," returned Tom.

"What then?" asked the young financial manager.

"An *airship!*" Tom exclaimed with such sudden energy that Ned started. "It just came to me!" explained the youthful inventor. "I was wondering how we could get the chemicals in from the top, and an airship is the solution. I can sail over the burning building and drop the chemicals down. That will douse the blaze if my plans go right."

Ned was silent a moment, considering Tom's daring plan and project. Then, as it became clearer, the young banker cried:

"Blamed if I don't think that's just the thing, Tom! It ought to work, and, if it does, it will save a lot of lives, to say nothing of property! A fire in a sky-scraper *ought* to be fought from above. Then the extinguisher element, whether chemicals or water, could be dropped where they'd do the most good. As it is now, with water, a lot of it is wasted. Some of it never reaches the heart of the fire, being splashed on the outside of the building. A lot more turns to steam before it hits the flames, and only a small percentage is really effective."

"That's my notion," Tom said.

"Then go ahead and do it!" urged his friend. "You have my permission!"

"Thanks," commented Tom dryly. "But there are several things to be worked out before we can start. I've got to devise some scheme for carrying a sufficient quantity of chemicals, and invent some way of releasing them from an airship over the blaze. But that last part ought to be easy, for I think I can alter my warfare bomb-dropping attachment to serve the purpose.

"What I really need, however, is some new chemical combination that will quickly put a really big blaze out of business. There are any number of these chemicals, but most of them depend on the production of carbon dioxide. This is the product of some solution of a carbonate and sulphuric acid, and I suppose, eventually, I'll work out something on that order. But I hope I may get something better."

"You haven't delved much into chemistry, have you?"

"No. And I wish now that I had. I see my limitations and realize my weakness. But I can brush up a little on my chemistry. As for the mechanical part, that of dropping the extinguisher on the blaze, I'm not worrying over that end."

"No," agreed Ned. "You have enough types of airships to be able to select just the best one for the purpose. But, say, Tom!" he suddenly cried, "why not ask him to help you?"

"Who?"

"Mr. Baxter. He's a chemist. And though he says his formulæ are about dyes and fireworks, maybe he can put you in the way of inventing a chemical solution that will be death to fires."

"He might," Tom agreed. "But I think he'll be out of business for some time. This shock— being overcome by smoke and his secret formulæ having been stolen—seem to have affected his mind. I don't know that I could depend on him."

"It's worth trying," declared Ned. "What do you suppose he means, Tom, saying that Field and Melling stole his formulæ?"

"Haven't the least idea. I only know those fireworks firm members slightly, if at all. I'm not sure I'd recognize them if I met them. But they are reputed to be wealthy, and I hardly think they would stoop to stealing some inventor's formulæ.

"We inventors are a suspicious lot, Ned, as you probably have found out," he added with a smile. "We imagine the rest of the world is out to cheat us, and I presume Josephus Baxter is no exception. Still, there may be some truth in his story. I'll give him all the help I can. But I'm going into the aerial fire-fighting game. I've been waiting for something new, and this may be it."

"You may count on me!" declared Ned. "And now, unless you're going to sit up all night and start studying chemistry, you'd better come to bed."

"That's right. To-morrow is another day. I hope Mr. Baxter gets some rest. Sleep will improve him a lot, the doctor said."

"I know one friend of yours who will be glad to know that you are going to start something," remarked Ned, as he and Tom started for their rooms, for the young manager was staying with his friend for the night.

"Who?" Tom wanted to know.

"Mr. Wakefield Damon," was the answer. "He hasn't been over lately, Tom."

"No, he's been off on a little trip, blessing everything from his baggage check to his suspender buttons," laughed the young inventor, as he recalled his eccentric acqaintance. "I shall be glad to see him again."

"He'll be right over as soon as he learns what's in the wind," predicted Ned.

The hopes that Mr. Baxter would be greatly improved in the morning were doomed to disappointment. He was in no actual danger, the doctor said, but his recovery from the effects of the smoke he had breathed was not as rapid as desired or hoped for.

"He's suffering from some shock," said the physician, "and his mental condition is against him. He ought to be kept quiet, and if you can't have him here, Mr. Swift, I can arrange to have him sent to a hospital."

"I wouldn't dream of it!" Tom exclaimed. "Let him stay here by all means. We have plenty of room, and Mrs. Baggert has been wishing for some one to nurse. Now she has him."

So it was arranged that the chemist should remain at the Swift home, and he gave a languid assent when they spoke to him of the matter. He really was much more ill than seemed at first.

But as everything possible had been done, Tom decided to go ahead with the new idea that had come to him—that of inventing an aerial chemical fire-fighting machine.

"And if we get a chance, Ned, we'll try to get back those secret formulæ Mr. Baxter claims to have lost," Tom declared. "I have heard some stories about that fireworks firm, which make me believe there may be something in Baxter's story."

"All right, Tom, I'm with you any time you need me," Ned promised.

The young inventor lost little time in beginning his operations. As he had said, the chief need was a fire extinguishing chemical solution or powder. Tom resolved to try the solution first, as it was easier to make. With this end in view he proceeded to delve into old and new chemistry books. He also sought the advice of his father.

And one day, when Ned called, Tom electrified his chum with the exclamation:

"Well, I'm going to give it a try!"

"What?"

"My aerial chemical fire-fighting apparatus. Of course I only have the chemical yet. I haven't worked on the carrying apparatus nor decided how I will attach it to an airship. But I'm going up now with some of my new solution and drop it on a blaze from above."

"Where are you going to get the fire?" asked Ned. "You can't have a sky-scraper blaze made to order, you know."

"No, but as this is only an experiment," Tom said, " a big bonfire will answer the purpose. I'm having Koku and Rad make one now down in our big meadow. As soon as it gets hot enough and fierce enough, I'll sail over it in my small machine, drop the extinguisher on it, and see what happens. Want to come?"

"Sure thing!" cried Ned. "And I hope the experiment is a success!"

"Thanks," murmured Tom. "I'm about ready to start. All I have to do is to take this tank up with me," and he pointed to one containing his new mixture. "Of course the arrangement for dumping it out of the aircraft is very crude," Tom said. "But I can work on that later."

Ned and he were busy putting the can of Tom's new chemical extinguisher in the airship when the door of the hangar was suddenly opened and a very much excited man entered crying:

"Fire! Fire! Bless my kitchen sink, your meadow's on fire, Tom Swift! It's blazing high! Fire! Fire!"

CHAPTER V

THE EXPLOSION

Tom and Ned were so startled by the entrance
of the excited man with his cry of "Fire!" that
the young inventor nearly dropped the tank of
liquid extinguisher he was helping to hoist into
the aeroplane. Then, as he caught sight of his
visitor, Tom exclaimed:

"Hello, Mr. Damon! We were wondering
whether you'd be along to witness our first experiment."

"Experiment, Tom Swift! Experiment! Bless
my Latin grammar! but you'd much better be
calling out the fire department to play on that
blaze down in your meadow. What is it—your
barns or one of your new shops?"

"Neither one, Mr. Damon," laughed Ned.
"It's only a blaze that Koku and Rad started."

"And the fire department is here," added Tom.

"Where?" inquired the eccentric man.

"Here," and Tom pointed to his airship—one
of the smaller craft—into which the tank of
chemicals had been hoisted.

"Oh!" exclaimed Mr. Damon. "Something new, eh, Tom?" His eyes glistened.

"Yes. Fighting fires from the air. I got the idea after the fireworks factory went up in smoke. Will you come along? There's plenty of room."

"I believe I will," assented Mr. Damon. It was not the first time, by any means, that he had gone aloft with Tom. "I happened to be coming over in my auto," he went on to explain, "when I happened to see the fire down in the meadow. I was afraid you didn't know about it."

"Oh, yes," replied Tom. "I had Rad and Koku light a big pile of packing boxes, to represent, as nearly as possible, on a small scale, a burning building. I plan now to sail over it and drop the tins of chemicals. They are arranged to burst as they fall into the blaze, and I hope the carbon dioxide set loose will blanket out the fire."

"Sounds interesting," commented Mr. Damon. "I'll go along."

The airship was wheeled out of the hangar and was soon ready for the flight. A big cloud of black vapor down in the meadow told Tom and Ned that Koku and Eradicate had done their work well. The giant and the colored man had poured oil over the wood to make a fierce blaze that would give Tom's new chemical combination a severe test.

A mechanic turned the propeller of the airship until there was an accumulation of gas in the different cylinders. Then he stepped back while Tom threw on the switch. This was not one of the self-starting types, of which Tom possessed one or two.

"Contact!" cried Tom sharply, and the man stepped forward to give the big blades a final turn that would start the motor. There was a muffled roar and then a steady staccato blending of explosions. Tom raced the motor while his men held the machine in place, and then, satisfied that all was well, the young inventor gave the word, and the craft raced over the ground, to soar aloft a little later.

Tom, Ned and Mr. Damon could look down to the meadow where the bonfire was blazing. A crowd had collected, but the heat of the blaze kept them at a good distance. Then, as many of the throng caught sight of the airship overhead, there was a new interest for them.

Tom had told Ned and Mr. Damon, before the trio had entered the machine, what he wanted them to do. This was to toss the chemicals overboard at the proper time. Of course in his perfected apparatus Tom hoped to have a device by which he could drop the fire extinguishing elements by a mere pressure of his finger or foot, as bombs were released from aircraft during the war. But this would serve for the time being.

Nearer and nearer the blaze the airship approached until it was almost above it. Tom had had some experience in bomb-dropping, and knew when to give the signal.

At last the signal came. Mr. Damon and Ned heaved over the side the metal containers of the powerful chemicals.

Down they went, unerring as an arrow, though on a slant, caused by the impetus given them by the speed of the airship.

Tom and his friends leaned over the side of the machine to watch the effect. They could see the chemicals strike the blaze, and it was evident from the manner in which the fire died down that the containers had broken, as Tom intended they should to scatter their contents.

"Hurray!" cried Ned, forgetting that he could not be heard, for no head telephones were used on this occasion and the roar of the motor would drown any human voice. "It's working, Tom!"

Truly the effect of the chemicals was seemingly to cause the fire to go out, but it was only a momentary dying down. Koku and Rad had made a fierce, yet comparatively small, conflagra-

tion, and though for a time the gas generated by
Tom's mixture dampened the blaze, in a few
seconds—less than half a minute—the flames
were shooting higher than ever.

Tom made a gesture of disappointment, and
swung his craft around in a sharp, banking turn.
He had no more chemicals to drop, as he had
thought this supply would be sufficient. However, he had guessed badly. The fire burned on,
doing no damage, of course, for that had been
thought of when it was started in the meadow.

"Something wrong!" declared the young inventor, when they were back at the hangar, climb-
ing out of the machine.

"What was it?" asked Ned.

"Didn't use the right kind of chemicals," Tom
answered. "From the way the flames shot up,
you'd think I had poured oil on the blaze instead
of carbon dioxide."

"Bless my insurance policy, Tom!" cried Mr.
Damon, "but I'd hate to trust to your apparatus
if my house caught."

"Don't blame you," Tom assented. "But I'll
do the trick yet! This is only a starter!"

During the next two weeks the young inventor
worked hard in his laboratory, Mr. Swift sometimes helping him, but more often Koku and
Eradicate. Mr. Baxter had recovered sufficiently

to leave the Swift home. But though the chemist seemed well physically, his mind appeared to be brooding over his loss.

"If I could only get my secret formulæ back!" he sighed, as he thanked Tom for his kindness. "I'm sure Field and Melling have them. And I believe they got them the night of the fireworks blaze; the scoundrels!"

"Well, if I can help you, please let me," begged Tom. And then he dismissed the matter from his mind in his anxiety to hit upon the right chemical mixture for putting out fires from the air.

One afternoon, at the end of a week in which he had been busily and steadily engaged on this work, Tom finally moved away from his laboratory table with a sigh of relief, and, turning to Eradicate, who had been helping him, exclaimed:

"Well, I think I have it now!"

"Good lan' ob massy, I hopes so!" exclaimed the colored man. "It sho' do smell bad enough, Massa Tom, to make any fire go an' run an' drown hisse'f! Whew-up! It's turrible stuff!"

"Yes, it isn't very pleasant," Tom agreed, with a smile. "Though I am getting rather used to it. But when it's in a metal tube it won't smell, and I think it will put out any fire that ever started. We'll give it a test now, Rad. Just take that flask of red stuff and pour it into this one of yellow. I'll go out and light the bonfire, and we'll make a small test."

Leaving Rad to mix some of the chemicals, a task the colored man had often done before, Tom went out into the yard near his laboratory to start a blaze on which his new mixture could be tested.

He had not got far from the laboratory door when he felt a sudden jar and a rush of air, and then followed the dull boom of an explosion. Like an echo came the voice of Eradicate:

"Oh, Massa Tom, I'se blowed up! It done sploded right in mah face!"

CHAPTER VI

TOM IS WORRIED

Dropping what he had in his hands, Tom Swift raced back to the laboratory where he had left Eradicate to mix the chemicals. Again the despairing, frightened cry of the colored man rang out.

"I hope nothing serious has happened," was the thought that flashed through Tom's mind. "But I'm afraid it has. I should have mixed those new chemicals myself."

Koku, the giant, who was at work in another part of the shop yard, heard Rad's cry and came running up. As there was always more or less jealousy between Eradicate and Koku, the latter now thought he had a chance to crow over his rival, not, of course, understanding what had happened.

"Ho! Ho!" laughed Koku. "You much better hab me work, Master Tom. I no make blunderstakes like dat black fellow! I never no make him!"

48

"I don't know whether Rad has made a mistake or not," murmured Tom. "Come along, Koku, we may need your help. There has been an explosion."

"Yep, dat Rad he don't as know any more as to blow up de whole place!" chuckled Koku.

He thought he would have a chance to make fun of Eradicate, but neither he nor Tom realized how serious had been the happening. As the young inventor reached the laboratory, which he had left but a few seconds before, he saw the interior almost in ruins. All about were scattered various pieces of apparatus, test tubes, alembics, retorts, flasks, and an electric furnace.

But what gave Tom more concern than anything else was the sight of Eradicate lying in the midst of broken glass on the floor. The colored man was moaning and held his hands over his face, and the young inventor could see that the hands, which had labored so hard and faithfully in his service, were cut and bleeding.

"Rad! Rad! what has happened?" cried Tom quickly.

"It sploded! It done sploded right in mah face!" moaned Eradicate. "I—I can't see no mo', Massa Tom! I can't see to help yo' nevah no mo'!"

"Don't worry about that, Rad!" cried Tom, as

cheerfully as possible under the circumstances. "We'll soon have you fixed up! Come in here, Koku, and help me carry Rad out!"

Though the fumes from the chemicals that had exploded were choking, causing both Tom and Koku to gasp for breath, they never hesitated. In they rushed and picked up the limp figure of the helpless colored man.

"Poor Rad!" murmured the giant Koku tenderly. "Him bad hurt! I carry him, Master Tom! I take him bed, an' I go for doctor! I run like painted pig!"

Probably Koku meant "greased pig," but Tom never thought of that. All his concern was for his faithful Eradicate.

"Me carry him, Master Tom!" cried Koku, all the petty jealousy of his rival passing away now. "Me take care ob Rad. Him no see, me see for him. Anybody hurt Rad now, got to hurt Koku first!"

It was a fine and generous spirit that the giant was showing, though Tom had no time to speculate on it just then.

"We must get him into the house, Koku," said the young inventor. "And two of us can carry him better than one. After we get him to a bed you can go for the doctor, though I fancy the telephone can run even quicker than you can, Koku."

"Whatever Master Tom say," returned the giant humbly, as he looked with pity at the suffering form of his rival—a rival no longer. It seemed that Rad's working days were over.

Tenderly the aged colored man was laid on a lounge in the living room, Mr. Swift and Mrs. Baggert hovering over him.

"Where are you worst hurt, Rad?" asked Tom, with a view to getting a line on which physician would be the best one to summon.

"It's all in mah face, Massa Tom," moaned the colored man. "It's mah eyes. Dat stuff done sploded right in 'em! I can't see—nevah no mo'!"

"Oh, I guess it isn't as bad as that," said Tom. But when he had a glimpse of the seared and wounded face of his faithful servant he could not repress a shudder.

A physician was summoned by telephone, and he arrived in his automobile at the same time that Mr. Damon reached Tom's house.

"Bless my bottle of arnica, Tom!" exclaimed the eccentric man, with sympathy in his voice. "What's this I hear? One of your men tells me old Eradicate is killed!"

"Not as bad as that, yet," replied Tom, as he came out, leaving the doctor to make his first examination. "It was an explosion of my new aerial fire-fighting chemicals that I left Rad to mix for me. If anything serious results to him from this I'll drop the whole business! I'll never forgive myself!"

"It wasn't your fault, Tom. Perhaps he did something wrong," said Mr. Damon.

"Yes, it was my fault. I should not have let him take the chance with a mixture I had tried only a few times. But we'll hope for the best. How is he, Doctor?" Tom asked a little later when the physician came out on the porch.

"He's doing as well as can be expected for the present," was the answer. "I have given him a quieting mixture. His worst injury seems to be to his face. His hands are cut by broken glass, but the hurts are only superficial. I think we shall have to get an eye specialist to look at him in a day or two."

"You mean that he—that he may go *blind?*" gasped Tom.

"Well, we'll not decide right away," replied the doctor, as cheerfully as he could. "I should rather have the opinion of an oculist before making that statement. It may be only temporary."

"That's bad enough!" muttered Tom. "Poor old Rad!"

"Me take care ob him," put in Koku, who had been humbly standing around waiting to hear the news. "Me never be mad at dat black man no more! Him my best friend! I lub him like I did my brudder!"

"Thank you, Koku," said Tom, and his mind went back to the time when he had escaped in his airship from the gigantic men, of whom Koku and his brother were two specimens. The brother had gone with a circus, and Koku, for several years, only saw him occasionally.

Everything possible was done for Eradicate, and the doctor said that it would be several days, until after the burns from the exploding chemicals had partly healed, before the eye-doctor could make an examination.

"Then we can only wait and hope," said Tom.

"And hope for the best!" advised Mr. Damon.

"I'll try," promised Tom. He went back to the laboratory with his eccentric friend and with Ned, who had come over as soon as he heard the news. Not much of an examination could be made, as the place was in such ruins. But it was surmised that in combining the two chemical mixtures a new one had been created, or at least one that Tom had not counted on. This had ex-

ploded, blowing Eradicate down, flaring a sheet
of flame up into his face, scattering broken glass
about, and generally creating havoc.

"I can't understand it," said Tom. "I was trying to make a fire *extinguishing* liquid, and it
turned out to be a fire *creator*. I don't see what
was wrong."

"One chemical might have been impure," suggested Ned.

"Yes," agreed Tom. "I'll check them over and
try to find out where the mistake happened."

"This place will have to be rebuilt," observed
Ned. "It's in bad shape, Tom."

"I don't mind that in the least, if Rad doesn't
lose his eyesight," was the answer of the young
inventor, and his friends could see that he was
much worried, as well he might be.

In silence Tom Swift looked about the ruins
of what had been a fine chemical laboratory.

"It will take a month to get this back in shape,"
he said ruefully. "I guess I shall have to post-
pone my experiments."

"Why not ask Mr. Baxter to help you?" suggested Ned.

"What can he do?" Tom wanted to know.
"He hasn't any laboratory."

"He has a sort of one," Ned rejoined. "You

know you told me to keep track of him and give him any help I could."

"Yes," Tom nodded.

"Well, the other day he came to me and said he had a chance to set up a small laboratory in a vacant shop near the river. He needed a little capital and I lent it to him, as you told me to."

"Glad you did," returned Tom. "But do you suppose his plant is large enough to enable me to work there until mine is in shape again?"

"It wouldn't do any harm to take a look," suggested Ned.

"I'll do it!" decided Tom, more hopefully than he had spoken since the accident.

CHAPTER VII

JOSEPHUS BAXTER seemed to have recovered some of his spirits after his narrow escape from death in the fireworks factory blaze. He greeted Tom and Ned with a smile as they entered the improvised laboratory he had been able to set up in what had once been a factory for the making of wooden ware, an industry that, for some reason, did not flourish in Shopton.

"I'm glad to see you, Mr. Swift," said the chemist, who seemed to have aged several years in the few weeks that had intervened since the fire. "I want to thank you for giving me a chance to start over again."

"Oh, that's all right," said Tom easily. "We inventors ought to help one another. Are you able to do anything here?"

"As much as possible without my secret formulæ," was the answer. "If I only had those back from the rascals, Field and Melling, I would be able to go ahead faster. As it is, I am work-

ing in the dark. For some of the formulæ were
given to me by a Frenchman, and I had only one
copy. I kept that in the safe of the fireworks
concern, and after the fire it could not be found."

"Was the safe destroyed?" asked Tom.

"No. But the doors were open, and much of
what had been inside was in ashes and cinders.
Amos Field claimed that the explosion had blown
open the safe and burned a lot of their valuable
fireworks formulæ too."

"And you believe they have yours?" asked Ned.

"I'm sure of it!" was the fierce answer.
"Those men are unprincipled rogues! They had
been at me ever since I was foolish enough to
tell them about my formulæ to get me to sell
them a share. But I refused, for I knew the
secret mixtures would make my fortune when I
could establish a new dye industry. Field and
Melling claimed they wanted the formulæ for
their fireworks, but that was only an excuse. The
formulæ were not nearly so valuable for pyro-
technics as for dyes. The fireworks business is
not so good, either, since so many cities have
voted for a 'Sane Fourth of July.'"

"I can appreciate that," said Tom. "But what
we called for, Mr. Baxter, is to find if you have
room enough to let me do a little experimenting
here. I am working on a new kind of fire ex-

tinguisher, to be dropped on tall buildings from an airship."

"Sounds like a good idea," said the chemist, rather dreamily.

"Well, I have the airship, and I can see my way clear to perfecting a device to drop the chemicals in metal tanks or bombs," went on Tom. "But what bothers me is the chemical mixture that will put out fires better than the carbon dioxide mixtures now on the market."

"I haven't given that much study myself," said Mr. Baxter. "But you are welcome to anything I have, Mr. Swift. The whole place, such as it is, will be at your disposal at any time. I intend to have it in better shape soon, but I have to proceed slowly, as I lost nearly everything I owned in that fire. If I could only get those formulæ back!" he sighed.

"Perhaps you may recall the combinations," suggested Ned. "Or can't you get them from that Frenchman?"

"He is dead," answered the chemist. "Everything seems to be against me!"

"Well, it's always darkest just before daylight," said Tom. "So let us hope for the best. We both have had a bit of bad luck. But when I think of Rad, who may lose his eyesight, I can stand my losses smiling."

"Yes," agreed Mr. Baxter, "you have big assets when you have your health and eyesight."

Three days later the eye specialist looked at Rad. Tom stood by anxiously and waited for the verdict. The doctor motioned to the young inventor to follow him out of the room, while Mrs. Baggert replaced the bandages on the colored man's eyes and Koku stood near him, sympathetically patting Rad on the back.

"Well?" asked Tom nervously, as he faced the physician.

"I am sorry, Mr. Swift, that I can not hold out much hope that your man will ever regain his sight," was the answer.

Tom could not repress a gasp of pity.

"I do not say that the case is altogether hopeless," the doctor went on; "but it would be wrong to encourage you to hope for much. I may be able to save partly the sight of one eye."

"Poor Rad!" murmured Tom. "This will break his heart."

"There is no need for telling him at once," Dr. Henderson said. "It will only make his recovery so much the slower. It will be weeks before I am able to operate, and, meanwhile, he should be kept as comfortable and cheerful as possible."

"We'll see to that," declared Tom. "Is he otherwise injured?"

"No, it is merely his eyesight that we have to fear for. And, as I said, that is not altogether hopeless, though it would not be honest to let you look for much success. I shall see him from time to time until his eyes are ready to operate on."

Tom and his friends were forced to take such comfort as they could from this verdict, but no hint of their downcast feelings were made manifest to Eradicate.

"Whut de doctor man done say, Massa Tom?" asked Eradicate when the young inventor went back into the sick room.

"Oh, he talked a lot of big Latin words, Rad— bigger words than you used to use on your mule Boomerang," and Tom forced a laugh. "All he meant was that you'd have to stay in bed a while and let Koku wait on you."

"Huh! Am dat—dat big—dat big *nice* man heah now?" asked Rad, feeling around with his bandaged hand; and a smile showed beneath the cloth over his eyes.

"I here right upsidedown by you, Rad," said Koku, and his big hand clasped the smaller one of the black man.

"Koku—yo'—yo' am mighty good to me," murmured Eradicate. "I reckon I been cross to yo' sometimes, but I didn't mean nuffin' by it!"

"Huh! me an' you good friends now," said the

giant. "Anybody what hurt my Rad, I—I—bust 'im! Dat I do!" cried the big fellow.

"Come on," whispered Tom to Ned. "They'll get along all right together now."

But Eradicate caught the sound of his young employer's footsteps and called:

"Yo' goin', Massa Tom?"

"Yes, Rad. Is there anything you want?"

"No, Massa Tom. I jest wanted to ast if yo' done 'membered de time mah mule Boomerang got stuck in de road, an' yo' couldn't git past in yo' auto? Does yo' 'member dat?"

"Indeed I do!" laughed Tom, and Eradicate also chuckled at the recollection.

"That laugh will do him more good than medicine," declared the doctor, as he took his leave. "I'll come again, when I can make a more thorough examination," he added.

For Tom the following days, that lengthened into weeks, were anxious ones. There was a constant worry over Eradicate. Then, too, he was having trouble with his latest invention—his aerial fire-fighting apparatus. It was not that Tom was financially dependent on this invention. He was wealthy enough for his needs from other patented inventions he and his father owned.

But Tom Swift was a lad not easily satisfied. Once embarked on an enterprise, whether it was

the creation of a gigantic searchlight, an electric
rifle, a photo telephone or a war tank, he never
rested until he had brought it to a successful con-
summation.

But there was something about this chemical
fire extinguishing mixture that defied the young
inventor's best efforts.   Mixture after mixture
was tried and discarded.   Tom wanted something
better than the usual carbonate and sulphuric
combination, and he was not going to rest until
he found it.

"I think you've struck a blind lead, Tom," said
Ned, more than once.

"Well, I'm not going to give up," was the firm
answer.

"Bless my shoe laces!" cried Mr. Damon, when
he had called on Tom once at the Baxter laboratory and had been driven out, holding his breath,
because of the chemical fumes, "I should think
you couldn't even start a fire with that around,
Tom, much less need to put one out."

"Well, it doesn't seem to work," said the young
inventor ruefully.   "Everything I do lately goes
wrong."

"It is that way sometimes," said Mr. Baxter.
"Suppose you let me study over your formulæ a
bit, Mr. Swift.   I haven't given much thought to
fire extinguishers, but I may be able, for that very

reason, to approach the subject from a new angle. I'll lay aside my attempt to get back the lost formulæ and help you."

"I wish you would!" exclaimed Tom eagerly. "My head is woozie from thinking! Suppose I leave you to yourself for a time, Mr. Baxter? I'll go for an airship ride."

"Yes, do," urged the chemist. "Sometimes a change of scene is of benefit. I'll see what I can do for you."

"Will you come along, Ned—Mr. Damon?" asked Tom, as he prepared to leave the improvised laboratory, the repairs on his own not yet having been finished.

"Thank you, no," answered Ned. "I have some collections to make."

"And I promised my wife I'd take her riding, Tom," said the jolly, eccentric man. "Bless my umbrella! she'd never forgive me if I went off with you. But I'll run you to your first stopping place, Ned, and you to your hangar, Tom."

His invitation was accepted, and, in due season, Tom was soaring aloft in one of his speedy cloud craft.

"Guess I'll drop down and get Mary Nestor," he decided, after riding about alone for a while and finding that the motor was running sweetly and smoothly. "She hasn't been out lately."

Tom made a landing in a field not far from the home of the girl he hoped to marry some day, and walked over to her house.

"Go for a ride? I just guess I will!" cried Mary, with sparkling eyes. "Just wait until I get on my togs."

She had a leather suit, as had Tom, and they were soon in the machine, which, being equipped with a self-starter, did not need the services of a mechanician to whirl the propellers.

"Oh, isn't it glorious!" said Mary, as she sat at Tom's side. They were in a little enclosed cabin of the craft—which carried just two—and, thus enclosed, they could speak by raising their voices somewhat, for the noise of the motor was much muffled, due to one of Tom's inventions.

Other rides on other days followed this one, for Tom found more rest and better refreshment after his hours of toil and study in these rides with Mary than in any other way.

"I do love these rides, Tom!" the girl cried one day when the two were soaring aloft. "And this one I really believe is better than any of the rest. Though I always think that," she added, with a slight laugh.

"Glad you like it," Tom answered, and there was something in his voice that caused Mary to look curiously at him.

"What's the matter, Tom?" she asked. "Has anything happened? Is Rad's case hopeless?"

"Oh, no, not yet. Of course it isn't yet sure that he will ever see again, but, on the other hand, it isn't decided that he can't. It's a fifty-fifty proposition."

"But what makes you so serious?"

"Was I?"

"I should say so! You haven't told me one funny thing that Mr. Damon has said lately."

"Oh, haven't I? Well, let me see now," and he sent the machine up a little. "Well, the other day he——"

Tom suddenly stopped speaking and began rapidly turning several valve wheels and levers.

"What—what's the matter?" gasped Mary, but she did not clutch his arm. She knew better than that.

"The motor has stopped," Tom answered, and the girl became aware of a cessation of the subdued hum.

"Is it—does it mean danger?" she asked.

"Not necessarily so," Tom replied. "It means we have to make a forced landing, that's all. Sit tight! We're going down rather faster than usual, Mary, but we'll come out of it all right!"

CHAPTER VIII

STRANGE TALK

THERE was a rapid and sudden drop. Mary, sitting beside Tom Swift in the speedy aeroplane, watched with fascinated eyes as he quickly juggled with levers and tried different valve wheels. The girl, through her goggles, had a vision of a landscape shooting past with the speed of light. She glimpsed a brook, and, almost instantly, they had skimmed over it.

A jar, a nerve-racking tilt to one side, the creaking of wood and the rattle of metal, a careening, and then the machine came to a stop, not exactly on a level keel, but at least right side up, in the midst of a wide field.

Tom shut off the gas, cut his spark, and, raising his goggles, looked down at Mary at his side.

"Scared?" he asked, smiling.

"I *was*," she frankly admitted. "Is anything broken, Tom?"

"I hope not," answered the young inventor. "At least if it is, the damage is on the under part.

Nothing visible up here. But let me help you out. Looks as if we'd have to run for it."

"Run?" repeated Mary, while proving that she did not exactly need help, for she was getting out of her seat unaided. "Why? Is it going to catch fire?"

"No. But it's going to rain soon—and hard, too, if I'm any judge," Tom said. "I don't believe I'll take a chance trying to get the machine going again. We'll make for that farmhouse and stay there until after the storm. Looks as if we could get shelter there, and perhaps a bit to eat. I'm beginning to feel hungry."

"It *is* going to rain!" decided Mary, as Tom helped her down over the side of the fusilage. "It's good we are so near shelter."

Tom did not answer. He was making a hasty but accurate observation of the state of his aeroplane. The landing wheels had stood the shock well, and nothing appeared to be broken.

"We came down rather harder than I wanted to," remarked Tom, as he crawled out after his inspection of the machine. "Though I've made worse forced landings than that."

"What caused it?" asked Mary, glancing up at the clouds, which were getting blacker and blacker, and from which, now and then, vivid flashes of lightning came while low mutterings of thunder rolled nearer and nearer.

"Something seemed to be wrong with the carburetor," Tom answered. "I won't try to mon-
key with it now. Let's hike for that farmhouse.
We'll be lucky if we don't get drenched. Are you
sure you're all right, Mary?"

"Certainly, Tom. I can stand a worse shaking
up than that. And you needn't think I can't run,
either!"

She proved this by hastening along at Tom's
side. And there was need of haste, for soon
after they left the stranded aeroplane the big
drops began to pelt down, and they reached the
house just as the deluge came.

"I don't know this place, do you, Tom?" asked
Mary, as they ran in through a gateway in a fence
that surrounded the property. A path seemed to
lead all around the old, rambling house, and there
was a porch with a side entrance door. This, being nearer, had been picked out by the young inventor and his friend.

"No, I don't remember being here before,"
Tom answered. "But I've passed the place often
enough with Ned and Mr. Damon. I guess they
won't refuse to let us sit on the porch, and they
may be induced to give us a glass of milk and
some sandwiches—that is, sell them to us."

He and Mary, a little breathless from their run,

hastened up on the porch, slightly wet from the sudden outburst of rain. As Tom knocked on the door there came a clap of thunder, following a burst of lightning, that caused Mary to put her hands over her ears.

"Guess they didn't hear that," observed Tom, as the echoes of the blast died away. "I mean my knock. The thunder drowned it. I'll try again."

He took advantage of a lull in the thundering reverberations, and tapped smartly. The door was almost at once opened by an aged woman, who stared in some amazement at the young people. Then she said:

"Guests must go to the front door."

"Guests!" exclaimed Tom. "We aren't exactly guests. Of course we'd like to be considered in that light. But we've had an accident —my aeroplane stopped and we'd like to stay here out of the storm, and perhaps get something to eat."

"That can be arranged—yes," said the old woman, who spoke with a foreign accent. "But you must go to the front door. This is the servant's entrance."

Mary was just thinking that they used considerable formality for casual wayfarers, when the situation dawned on Tom Swift.

"Is this a restaurant—an inn?" he asked.

"Yes," answered the old woman. "It is Meadow Inn. Please go to the front door."

"All right," Tom agreed good-naturedly. "I'm glad we struck the place, anyhow."

The porch extended around three sides of the old, rambling house. Proceeding along the sheltered piazza, Tom and Mary soon found themselves at the front door. There the nature of the place was at once made plain, for on a board was lettered the words "Meadow Inn."

"I see what has happened," Tom remarked, as he opened the old-fashioned ground glass door and ushered Mary in. "Some one has taken the old farmhouse and made it into a roadhouse—a wayside inn. I shouldn't think such a place would pay out here; but I'm mighty glad we struck it."

"Yes, indeed," agreed Mary.

The old farmhouse, one of the best of its day, had been transformed into a roadhouse of the better class. On either side of the entrance hall were dining rooms, in which were set small tables, spread with snowy cloths.

"In here, sir, if you please," said a white-aproned waiter, gliding forward to take Tom's leather coat and Mary's jacket of like material. The waiter ushered them into a room, in which at first there seemed to be no other diners. Then, from behind a screen which was pulled around a table in one corner, came the murmur of voices and the clatter of cutlery on china, which told of some one at a meal there.

"Somebody is fond of seclusion," thought Tom, as he and Mary took their places. And as he glanced over the bill of fare his ears caught the murmur of the voices of two men coming from behind the screen. One voice was low and rumbling, the other high-pitched and querulous.

"Talking business, probably," mused Tom. "What do you feel like eating?" he asked Mary.

"I wasn't very hungry until I came in," she answered, with a smile. "But it is so cozy and quaint here, and so clean and neat, that it really gives one an appetite. Isn't it a delightful place, Tom? Did you know it was here?"

"It is very nice. And as this is the first I have been here for a long while I didn't know, any more than you, that it had been made into a road-house. But what shall I order for you?"

"I should think you would have had enough experience by this time," laughed Mary, for it was not the first occasion that she and Tom had dined out.

Thereupon he gave her order and his own, too, and they were soon eating heartily of food that was in keeping with the appearance of the place.

"I must bring Ned and Mr. Damon here," said Tom. "They'll appreciate the quaintness of this inn," for many of the quaint appointments of the old farmhouse had been retained, making it a charming resort for a meal.

"Mr. Damon will like it," said Mary. "Especially the big fireplace," and she pointed to one on which burned a blaze of hickory wood. "He'll bless everything he sees."

"And cause the waiter to look at me as though I had brought in an escaped inmate from some sanitarium," laughed Tom. "No use talking, Mr. Damon is delightfully queer! Now what do you want for dessert?"

"Let me see the card," begged Mary. "I fancy some French pastry, if they have it."

Tom gazed idly but approvingly about as she scanned the list. The sound of the rumbling and the higher-pitched voices had gone on throughout the entire meal, and now, as comparative silence filled the room, the clatter of knives and forks having ceased, Tom heard more clearly what was being said behind the screen.

"Well, I tell you what it is," said the man whom Tom mentally dubbed Mr. High. "We got out of that blaze mighty luckily!"

"Yes," agreed he of the rumbly voice, whom

Tom thought of as Mr. Low, "it was a close shave. If it hadn't been for his chemicals, though, there would have been a cleaner sweep."

"Indeed there would! I never knew that any of them could act as fire extinguishers."

Tom seemed to stiffen at this, and his hearing became more acute.

"They aren't really fire extinguishers in the real sense of the word," went on the other man behind the screen. "It must have been some accidental combination of them. But in spite of that we put it all over Josephus Baxter in that fire!"

"What's this? What's this?" thought Tom, shooting a glance at Mary and noting that apparently she had not heard what was said. "What strange talk is this?"

CHAPTER IX

"WHAT'S that?" exclaimed Mary Nestor, giving such a start as she sat opposite Tom at the restaurant table that she dropped the bill of fare she had been looking over.

A crash had resounded through the room, but it spoke well for the state of Tom's nerves that he gave no indication that he had heard the noise. It was caused by a waiter when he dropped a plate, which was smashed into pieces on the floor. The noise was startling enough to excuse Mary for jumping in her chair, and it seemed to put an end to the strange talk of "Mr. High" and "Mr. Low" back of the screen, for after the crash of china only indistinct murmurs came from there. But Tom Swift did not cease to wonder at the import of the talk about chemicals, fire, and the mention of the name of Josephus Baxter.

"I think I'll try some of those Murolloas, as they call them, Tom," announced Mary, having made her selection of the pastry. "And may I have another cup of tea?"

74

"Two if you like," answered the young inventor. "They say tea is good for the nerves, and you seem to need something, judging by the way you jumped when that plate fell."

"Oh, Tom, that isn't fair! After the way we had to come down in your 'plane!" objected Mary.

"That's right!" he conceded. "I forgot about that. My fault, entirely!"

Mary smiled, and seemed to have regained her composure. Tom glanced at her anxiously, not because of what he thought might be the state of her nerves, but to see if she had sensed anything the two men behind the screen had said. But the girl gave no indication that her mind had been occupied with anything more than the selection of her dessert.

"I wonder who they are, and what they meant by that talk," mused Tom, as the waiter served the Murolloas to him and Mary. "Poor Baxter! It looks as if he might have more enemies than the fireworks men he accuses of having taken his valuable formulæ. I must see him soon, and have a talk with him. Yes, I must make a special point to see Josephus Baxter. But first I'd like to have a glimpse of these men."

Tom's wish in this respect was soon gratified, for before he and Mary had finished their pastry and tea there was a scraping of chairs back of the sheltering screen, and the two men, "Mr. Low" and "Mr. High," who had finished their meal, came forth.

Tom's judgment as to the statures of the men, based on the quality of their voices, was not exactly borne out. For it was the big man who had the high pitched, squeaky voice, and the little man who had the deep, rumbling tones.

They passed out, without more than a glance at Tom and his companion, but the young inventor peered at them sharply. As far as he could tell he had seen neither of them before, though he had an idea of their identity.

Tom took the chance to make certain this conjecture when Mary left her seat, announcing that she was going to the ladies' parlor to arrange her hair, which the run to escape from the rain had disarranged.

"Some storm," Tom observed to the waiter, who came up when the young inventor indicated that he wanted his check.

"Yes, sir, it came suddenly. Hope you didn't have to change a tire in it, sir."

"No, my machine isn't that kind," replied Tom, as he handed out a generous tip. "If I need a new tire I generally need a whole new outfit."

"Oh, then——" Obviously the man was puzzled.

"We came in an aeroplane," Tom explained. "But we had to make a forced landing. Is there a garage near here? I may need some help getting started."

"We accommodate a few cars in what was once the barn, and we have a good mechanic, sir. If you'd like to see him——"

"I would," interrupted Tom. "Tell the young lady to wait here for me. I'll see if I can get the *Scud* to work. If not, I'll have to telephone to town for a taxi. Did those men who just left come in a car?" and he nodded in the direction taken by the two who had dined behind the screen.

"Yes, sir. And they had engine trouble, I believe. Our man fixed up their machine."

"Then he's the chap I want to see," thought Tom. "I'll have a talk with him." He reasoned that he could get more about the identity of the two mysterious men from the mechanic than from the waiter. Nor was he wrong in this surmise.

"Oh, them two fellers!" exclaimed the mechanician, after he had agreed to go with Tom to where the airship *Scud* was stalled. "They come from over Shopton way. They own a fireworks factory—or they did, before it burned."

"Are they Field and Melling?" asked Tom, trying not to let any excitement betray itself in his voice.

"That's the names they gave me," said the man. "Little man's Field. He gave me his card. I'm going to get a job overhauling his car. There isn't enough work here to keep a man busy, and I told 'em I could do a little on the outside. This place just started, and not many folks know about it yet."

"So I judge," Tom said. "Well, I'll be glad to have you give me a hand. I fancy the carburetor is out of order."

And this, when the young inventor and the mechanician from Meadow Inn reached the stranded *Scud,* was found to be the case. The storm had passed, and Mary told Tom she would not mind waiting at the Inn until he found whether or not he could get his air craft in working order.

"There you are! That's the trouble!" exclaimed the mechanician, as he took something out of the carburetor. "A bit of rubber washer choked the needle valve."

"Glad you found it," said Tom heartily. "Now I guess we can ride back."

While preparations were being made to test the *Scud* after the carburetor had been reassembled, Tom's mind was busy with many thoughts, and chief among them were suspicions concerning Field and Melling.

"If their talk meant anything at all," reasoned the young inventor, "it meant that there was some deal in which Josephus Baxter got the worst of it. 'Putting it over on him in the fire,' could only mean that. Of course it isn't any of my business, in a way, but I don't think it is right to stand by and see a fellow inventor defrauded.

"Of course," mused Tom, while his helper put the finishing touches to the carburetor, "it may have been a business deal in which one took as many chances as the other. There are always two sides to every story. Baxter says they took his formulæ, but he may have taken something from them to make it even. The only thing is that I'd trust Baxter sooner than I would those two fellows, and he certainly had a narrow squeak at the fire.

"But I have my own troubles, I guess, trying to perfect that fire-fighting chemical, and I haven't much time to bother with Field and Melling, unless they come my way."

"There, I reckon she'll work," said the mechanician, as he fastened the last valve in the carburetor. "It was an easier job than I expected. Wasn't as much trouble as I had over their car— those two fellers you were speaking of—Field and Melling. They're rich guys!"

"Yes?" replied Tom, questioningly.

"Sure! They've started a big dye company."

"A dye company?" repeated the young inventor, all his suspicions coming back as he recalled that Baxter had said his formulæ were more valuable for dyes than for fireworks.

"Yes, they're trying to get the business that used to go to the Germans before the war," went on the man.

"Yes, the Germans used to have a monopoly of the dye industry," said Tom, hoping the man would talk on. He need not have worried. He was of the talkative type.

"Well, if these fellers have their way they'll make a million in dyes," proceeded the mechanician, as he stepped down out of the airship. "They've built a big plant, and they have offices in the Landmark Building."

"Where's that?" asked Tom.

"Over in Newmarket," the man went on, naming the nearest large city to Shopton. "The Landmark Building is a regular New York skyscraper. Haven't you seen it?"

"No," Tom answered, "I haven't. Been too busy, I guess. So Field and Melling have their offices there?"

"Yes, and a big plant on the outskirts for making dyes. They half offered me a job at the fac-

tory, but I thought I'd try this out first; I like it
here."

"It is a nice place," agreed Tom. "Well, now
let's see if she'll work," and he nodded at the
Scud.

It needed but a short test to demonstrate this,
and soon Tom went back to the Inn for Mary.

"Are you sure we shall not have to make another forced landing?" she asked with a smile, as
she took her place in the cockpit.

"You can't guarantee anything about an aeroplane," said Tom. "But everything is in our
favor, and if we do have to come down I have a
better landing field than this." He glanced over
the meadow near the wayside inn.

"I suppose I'll have to take a chance," said
Mary.

However, neither of them need have worried,
for the *Scud* tried, evidently, to redeem herself,
and flew back to Shopton without a hitch. After
making sure that his engine was running
smoothly, Tom found his mind more at ease, and
again he caught himself casting about to find
some basis for his suspicious thoughts regarding
the two men who had talked behind the screen.

"What is their game?" Tom found himself
asking himself over and over again. "What did
they 'put over' on poor Baxter?"

Tom had a chance to find out more about this, or at least start on the trail sooner than he expected. For when he landed he saw Koku, the giant, coming toward him with an appearance of excitement.

"Is Rad worse? Is there more trouble with his eyes?" asked the young inventor.

"No, him not much too bad," answered Koku. "I keep him good as I can. He sleep now, so I come out to swallow some fresh air. But man come to see you—much mad man."

"Mad?" queried Tom.

"Well, what you say—angry," went on Koku. "Man what was in Roman Skycracker blaze."

"Oh, you mean Mr. Baxter, who was in the fireworks blaze," translated Tom. "Where is he, and what's the matter?"

CHAPTER X

ANOTHER ATTEMPT

Koku managed to make Tom understand that the dye inventor was in the main office of the Swift plant talking to Tom's father. The young inventor sent Mary home in his electric runabout in company with Ned Newton, who, fortunately, happened along just then, and hurried to his office.

"Oh, Tom, I'm glad you have arrived," said his father. "You remember Mr. Baxter, of course."

"I should hope so," Tom answered, extending his hand. He noticed that the man whom he had helped save from the fireworks blaze was under the stress of some excitement.

"I hope he hasn't been getting on dad's nerves," thought Tom, as he took a seat. The elder Mr. Swift had been quite ill, and it was thought for a time that he would have to give up helping Tom. But there had been a turn for the better, and the aged inventor had again taken his place in the laboratory, though he was frail.

"What's the trouble now?" asked Tom. "At

least I assume there has been some trouble," he
went on. "If I am wrong——"

"No, you are right, unfortunately," said Mr.
Baxter gloomily. "The trouble is that everything I do is a failure. Up to a little while ago
I thought I might succeed, in spite of Field and
Melling's theft of the formulæ from me. I
made a purple dye the other day, and tested it to-
day. It was a miserable failure, and it got on my
nerves. I came to see if you could help me."

"In what way?" asked Tom, wondering
whether or not he had best tell Mr. Baxter what
he had overheard at the Inn.

"Well, I need better laboratory facilities," the
man went on. "I know you have been very kind
to me, Mr. Swift, and it seems like an imposi-
tion to ask for more. But I need a different lot
of chemicals, and they cost money. I also need
some different apparatus. You have it in your
big laboratory. That wouldn't cost you anything. But of course to go out and buy what I
need——"

"Oh I guess we can stand that, can't we, Dad?"
asked Tom, with a genial smile. "You may have
free access to our big laboratory, Mr. Baxter, and
I'll see that you get what chemicals you need."

"Oh, thank you!" exclaimed the inventor.
"Now I believe I shall succeed in spite of those

rascals. Just think, Mr. Swift! They have started a big new dye factory."

"So I have heard," replied Tom.

"And I'm almost sure they're using the secret formulæ they stole from me!" exclaimed Mr. Baxter. "But I'll get the best of them yet! I'll invent a better dye than they ever can, even if they use the secrets the old Frenchman gave me. All I need is a better place to work and all the chemicals at my disposal."

"Then we'll try to help you," offered Tom.

"And if I can do anything let me know," put in Mr. Swift. "I shall be glad to get in the harness again, Tom!" he added.

"Well, if you're so anxious to work, Dad, why not give me a hand with my fire extinguisher chemical?" asked Tom. "I haven't been able to hit on the solution, somehow or other."

"Perhaps I may be able to give you a hint or two after I get settled down," suggested Mr. Baxter.

"I shall be glad of any assistance you can give," replied Tom Swift. "And now I'm going to start right in. Dad, you can make the arrangements for Mr. Baxter to use our big laboratory. And let him have credit for any chemicals he needs. Have them put on my bill, for I am buying a lot myself."

"I'll never forget this," said Mr. Baxter, and there were tears in his eyes as he shook hands with Tom, who tried to make light of his generous act.

Tom, after the wrecking of his laboratory, in which accident poor Eradicate was injured, had built himself another—two others, in fact, after having shared Mr. Baxter's temporary one for a time. Tom put up the most completely equipped laboratory that could be devised, and he also erected a smaller one for his own personal use, the main one being at the disposal of his father and the various heads of the different departments of the Shopton plant.

The little conference broke up, and Tom was on his way to his own special private laboratory when there came the sound of some excitement in the corridor outside and Mr. Damon burst in.

"Bless my accident policy, Tom! what's this I hear?" he asked, all in a fluster.

"I'm sure I don't know," answered the young inventor, with a smile. "What about?"

"About you and Mary Nestor being killed!" burst out Mr. Damon. "I heard you fell in the aeroplane and were both dashed to pieces!"

"If you can believe the evidence of your own eyes, I'm far from being in that state," laughed

Tom. "And as for Mary, she just left here with Ned Newton."

"Thank goodness!" sighed Mr. Damon, sinking into a chair. "Bless my elevator! I rushed over as soon as I heard the news, and I was almost afraid to come in. I'm so glad it didn't happen!"

"No gladder than I," said Tom. "We had to make a forced landing, that was all," and he made as light of the incident as possible when he saw the look of terror in his father's eyes.

"Some people in Waterford saw you going down," went on Mr. Damon, "and they told me."

"It was a false alarm," replied Tom. "And now, Mr. Damon, if you want to smell some perfumes come with me."

"Are you going into that line, Tom?" asked the eccentric man. "Bless my handkerchief, my wife will be glad of that!"

"I mean I'm going to experiment some more with fire-extinguishing chemicals," laughed the young inventor. "If you want to——"

"Bless my gas mask, I should say *not!*" cried Mr. Damon. "I don't see how you stand those odors, Tom Swift."

"Guess I'm used to 'em," was the answer. And then, leaving his father to entertain Mr. Damon and to make arrangements for Mr. Baxter's use of the main laboratory, he betook himself to his own private quarters.

The next week or so was a busy time for Tom; so busy, in fact, that he had little chance to see Mr. Baxter. All he knew was that the unfortunate man was also laboring in his own line, and Tom wished him success. He knew that if the man made any discoveries that would help with the fire-extinguishing fluid he would report, as he had promised.

"Well, Tom, how goes it?" asked Ned one day when he came over to call on his chum. "Are you ready to accept contracts for putting out skyscraper blazes in all big cities?"

"Not yet," was the answer. "But I'm going to make another attempt, Ned."

"You mean another experiment?"

"Yes, I have evolved a new combination of chemicals, using something of the carbonate idea as a basis. I found that I couldn't get away from that, much as I wanted to. But my application is entirely new, at least I hope it will prove so."

"When are you going to try it?" asked Ned.

"Right away. All I have to do is to put the chemicals in the metal tank."

"Then I'd better get my leather suit on," remarked Ned, starting to take off his street coat.

Tom kept for his chum a full outfit of flying garments, one suit being electrically heated.

"Oh, we aren't going up in any airship," Tom said.

"Why, I thought you were going to test your aerial fire fighting dingus!" exclaimed Ned.

"So I am. But I want to stay on the ground and watch the effect on the blaze as the tank bursts and scatters the chemical fluid."

"Then you want me, and perhaps Mr. Damon, to take the stuff up in the machine? Excuse me. I don't believe I care to run an airship myself."

"No," went on Tom, "there isn't any question of an airship this time. No one is going up. Come on out into the yard and I'll show you."

Ned Newton followed his chum out into the big yard near one of the shops. Erected in it, and evidently a new structure, was a large wooden scaffold in square tower shape with a long overhanging arm and a platform on the extremity. Beneath it was a pit dug in the earth, and in this pit, which was directly under the outstanding arm of the tower, was a pile of wood and shavings, oil-soaked.

"Oh, I see the game," remarked Ned. "You're going to drop the stuff from this height instead of doing it from an airship."

"Yes," Tom answered. "There will be time

enough to go on with the airship end of it after I get the right combination of chemicals. And by having a metal container with the stuff in dropped from this frame work, I can station myself as near the burning pit as I can get and watch what happens."

"It's a good idea," decided Ned. "I wonder you didn't try that before."

"Mr. Baxter suggested it," replied Tom. "That helpful idea more than pays me for what I have done for him. So now, if you're ready, I'd like to have you watch with me and make some notes, one of us on one side of the pit, and one on the other. There are always two sides to a fire, the leeward and the windward, and I want to see how my chemicals act in both positions."

"I'm with you," said Ned. "Who's going to drop the stuff—Koku?"

"No, he is a bit too heavy for the frame work, which I had put up in a hurry. I'd have Rad do it, but he's out of the game."

"Poor old Rad!" murmured Ned. "Do you think he'll ever get better, Tom?"

"I don't know," sighed the young inventor. "All I can do is to hope. He is very patient, and Koku is devoted to him. All their little bickerings and squabbles seem to have been forgotten."

Tom called some of his workmen, some of

them to start the blaze of inflammable material in
the pit, while one climbed up to the top of the
tower of scantlings and made his way out on the
extended arm, where there was a little platform
for him to stand until it was time to drop the
chemicals.

"Light her up!" cried Tom Swift, and a match
was thrown in among the oiled wood. In an
instant a fierce blaze shot up, as hot, in proportion, as would come from any burning building.

For the second time Tom was about to make a
test on a fairly large scale of his experimental
extinguisher mixture.

"All ready up there?" he called to his helper
perched high in the air.

"All ready!" came back the answer above the
roar and crackle of the flames that made Tom and
Ned step back.

Would success or failure attend the young inventor's project?

CHAPTER XI

THE BLAZING TREE

Tom Swift hesitated a moment before giving the final word that would send the metal container of powerful chemicals down into the midst of the crackling flames. He wanted to make sure, in his own mind, that he had done everything possible to insure the success of his undertaking. The young inventor never attempted the solution of any problem without going into it with his whole energy. So he wanted this experiment to succeed.

He quickly reviewed, mentally, the composition of the chemical compound. He had made it as strong as possible, and he had spared no pains to insure a hot fire, so that the test would not be too simple.

"What's the matter, Tom?" asked Ned, as his chum appeared to hesitate about giving the word that would send the chemicals hurtling down into the fire.

"Nothing. I was just making sure I hadn't

forgotten anything," Tom answered. "I guess I haven't."

He paused a moment, looked up at his assistant on the overhanging arm of the tower, glanced down at the flames, now at their height, and then suddenly cried:

"Let her go!"

"Right!" came back the man's voice, and then a dark object, like a bomb, was seen descending from the skeleton framework above the flames.

There was a scattering of the fire in the pit as the extinguisher bomb fell among the blazing embers. Then followed a slight explosion when the bomb broke, as it was intended it should.

Tom and Ned leaned forward to peer through the pall of smoke which swirled this way and that. Here was to come the real test of the device. Would the fumes of the liberated chemicals choke the fire, or would it burn on in spite of them? That was the question to be settled for Tom Swift.

Almost immediately he had his answer. For after a fierce burst of the tongues of fire following the fall of the bomb, there was a distinct dying down of the conflagration in the pit. Great clouds of smoke arose, but the fire was quenched in a great measure, and as the fire-blanketing gas continued to be generated from the chemicals liberated from the bomb, there was a further dying down of the crackling fire.

"Tom, you've struck it!" yelled Ned in delight. "You have the right combination this time!"

Tom did not answer. He leaned forward and looked eagerly down into the pit. He was about to join with Ned in agreeing that he had, indeed, solved the problem, when, to his surprise, the flames started up again.

"What's this?" asked the young financial manager. "Are you going to have a second test, Tom?"

"Not that I know of," was the puzzled answer. "I don't exactly understand this myself, Ned. By all calculations this fire ought to have died a natural death, but now it is breaking out again. I think what must have happened is that a quantity of the oil they poured on collected in a pool and didn't get all the effects of the chemicals from the bomb. Then the oil started to blaze."

"What can you do about it?" Ned wanted to know.

"Oh, I've got another bomb up there," and Tom pointed to his helper who was still perched on the overhanging arm. "I was prepared for some such emergency as this. Drop the other one!" Tom yelled, and again a dark object fell,

bursting in the pit and again liberating the gas
that was supposed to choke any fire.

The flames that had started up for the second
time instantly died down, and Ned, leaning over
the edge of the pit, cried:

"Hurray, Tom! That does the business!"

But the young inventor shook his head.

"I'm not quite satisfied," he remarked. "It
didn't work quickly enough. What I want is a
chemical combination that will choke the fire off
first shot."

"Well, you pretty nearly have it," observed
Ned.

"Yes. But 'good enough' isn't what I want,"
Tom said. "I've got to work on that chemical
compound again. I think I know where I can
improve it."

"Well, if I were a fire, and I had this happen
to me," remarked Ned, laughing and pointing to
the heap of blackened embers in the pit, "I should
feel very much discouraged."

"But not enough," declared Tom. "I want
the fire to be out more quickly than this one was.
I think I can improve that chemical compound,
and I'm going to do it."

"All right! Come on down!" he called to his
helper, who was still perched on the overhanging
arm. "We won't do any more to-day."

"What is your next move?" asked Ned, as Tom started for his small, private laboratory.

"Oh, I'm going to fiddle around among those sweet-smelling chemicals," answered the young inventor.

"Bless my vest buttons! then I'm not coming in," exclaimed a voice which could proceed from none other than Mr. Damon. And he it proved to be. He had driven over from Waterford in his automobile and had arrived just as the fire test was concluded.

"Oh, come on in!" called Tom. "You can visit with dad, and Eradicate will be glad to see you."

"Poor Rad! How is he?" asked Mr. Damon, walking along with Tom and Ned.

"No change," was the sad answer of the young inventor, for he felt responsible for the mishap to the colored man. "They can't operate on his eyes yet."

"And when they do will he be able to see?" asked Mr. Damon.

"That is what we are all hoping," answered Tom with a sigh. "But do go in to see him, Mr. Damon. It will cheer him up."

"I will," promised the eccentric man. "At any rate I'll not venture near your perfume shop, Tom Swift!"

"And I don't see that I can be of any service," added Ned, "so I'm off to my work."

"All right," assented Tom. "I've got several new schemes to try. Some of them ought to work."

Tom Swift was very busy for the next few days—so busy, in fact, that even Mary saw little of him. He was closeted with Mr. Baxter more than once, and that individual seemed to lose some of his bitter feelings over the loss of his formulæ as he found he could be of service to the young inventor. For he was of service in suggesting new ways of combining fire-fighting chemicals, gained by his association with the fire-works concern.

"And that's about all the benefit I derived from being with those scoundrels, Field and Melling," said Mr. Baxter gloomily.

"You still think they took your dye formulæ?" asked Tom.

"I'm positive of it, but I can't prove anything. They threatened to get the best of me when I would not sell them, for a ridiculously low sum, an interest in the secrets. And I believe they did get the best of me during that fire."

"I believe the same!" exclaimed Tom.

"How is that? What do you know? Can

you help me prove anything against them?" eagerly asked the chemist.

"Well, I don't know," answered Tom slowly. "I'll tell you what I heard."

Thereupon he related the conversation he had overheard while with Mary at the wayside inn. The eyes of Josephus Baxter gleamed as he listened to this recital.

"So that was their game!" he cried, as he smote the table with his fist, thereby nearly upsetting a test tube of acid, which Tom caught just in time. "I knew something crooked was going on, and they thought I'd be so badly overcome in the fire that I wouldn't know, or wouldn't remember, what happened."

"What did happen?" asked Tom. "All I know is that you were overcome in the laboratory room."

"It's too long a story to tell in detail now," said Mr. Baxter. "But the main facts are that through misrepresentations I was induced to associate myself with Field and Melling. They had a good factory for the making of fireworks, and some of the chemicals used in that industry also enter into the manufacture of the kind of dyes I have in mind to make. So I associated myself with them, they agreeing to let me use their laboratory.

"One night they came to see me as I was working there over my formulæ. They pretended to have discovered something in an expired patent that nullified what I had. I did not believe this to be so, and I brought out my formulæ to compare with theirs—or what they said they had. The next thing I remember was that the fire broke out and my formulæ disappeared. Then I was overcome, and I did not care what happened to me, for, having lost the valuable dye formulæ, I did not think life worth living.

"Perhaps I was foolish," said Mr. Baxter, "but I had tried so many things and failed, and I counted so much on these formulæ that it seemed as if the bottom dropped out of everything when I lost them."

"I know," said Tom sympathetically. "I've been in the same boat myself. But are you sure they took the papers which meant so much to you?"

"I don't see who else could," answered the chemist. "The papers were in a tin box on the table in the room where I was overcome by fire gases, or where, perhaps, they drugged me. I am not clear on this point. And afterward the tin box could not be found. There wasn't enough fire in that room to have melted it."

"No," agreed Tom, "it was mostly smoke in

there, and smoke won't melt tin. Nor did I see any box on the table when we carried you out."

"Then the only other surmise is that Field and Melling got away with my formulæ during the excitement and when I was half unconscious," went on Mr. Baxter bitterly. "But you can see how foolish I would be to accuse them in court. I haven't a bit of proof."

"Not much, for a fact," agreed Tom. "Well, with what I heard and what you tell me, perhaps we can work up a case against them later. I'll go over it with Ned. He has a better head for business than I."

"Yes, we inventors need some business brains; or at least the time to give to business problems," agreed the chemist. "But enough of my troubles. Let's get at this chemical compound of yours."

Tom and Mr. Baxter spent many days and nights perfecting the fire-extinguisher chemical, and, after repeated tests, Tom felt that he was nearer his goal.

One afternoon Ned called, and Tom invited him to go for a ride in a small but speedy aeroplane.

"Anything special on?" asked the young manager.

"In a way, yes," Tom answered. "I'm having a firm in Newmarket make me some different containers, and they have promised me samples to-day. I thought I'd take a fly over and get them. I have the chemical compound all but perfected now, and I want to give it another test."

"All right, I'm with you," assented Ned. "Newmarket," he added musingly. "Isn't that where Field and Melling are now?"

"Yes. They have a factory on the outskirts of the place, and their offices are in the Land-mark Building. But we aren't going to see them, though we may call on them later, when you have that case better worked up." For Ned's services had been enlisted to aid Mr. Baxter.

"I shall need a little more time," remarked Ned. "But I think we can at least bluff them into playing into our hands. I have a report to hear from a private detective I have hired."

"I hope we can do something to aid Baxter," remarked Tom. "He has done me good service in this chemical fire extinguisher matter."

A little later Tom and Ned were speeding through the air on their way to Newmarket. The rapid flier was making good time at not a great height when Ned, leaning forward, appeared to be gazing at something in the near distance.

"What's the matter?" asked Tom, for he had his silencer on this craft and it was possible for the occupants to converse. "Do you hear one of the cylinders missing, Ned?"

"No. But what's that smoke down there?" and Ned pointed. "It looks like a fire!"

"It is a fire!" exclaimed Tom, as he took an observation. "Not a big one, but a fire, just the same. If only——"

He did not finish what he started to say, but changed the direction of his air craft and headed directly toward a pall of smoke about a mile away.

In a few seconds they were near enough to make out the character of the blaze.

"Look, Tom!" cried Ned. "It's an immense tree on fire!"

"A tree!" exclaimed Tom, half incredulously, for he was leaning forward to look at one of the aeroplane gages and did not have a clear view of what Ned was looking at.

"Yes, as sure as Mr. Damon would bless something if he were here! It's a tree on fire up near the top!"

"That's strange!" murmured Tom. "But it may give me just the chance I've been looking for."

Ned wondered at this remark on the part of his chum as the airship drew nearer the blazing monarch in the patch of woods over which they were then hovering.

CHAPTER XII

TOM IS LONESOME

"This is certainly the strangest sight I ever saw," remarked Ned, as he and his chum flew nearer and nearer to the smoking and blazing tree. "Is the world turning upside down, Tom, when fires start in this fashion?"

"I fancy it can easily be explained," answered the young inventor. "We'll go into that later. Here, Ned, grab hold of that tin can on the floor and take out the screw plug."

"What's the idea?"

"I want you to drop it as nearly as you can right into the midst of the tree that's on fire."

"Oh, I get your drift! Well, you can count on me."

Ned picked up from the floor of their aeroplane a metal can similar to those Tom used to hold oil or perhaps spare gasoline when he was experimenting on airship speed. The opening was closed with a screw plug, with wings to afford an easier grip. As Ned unscrewed this his nostrils were greeted by an odor that made him gasp.

"Don't mind a little thing like that," cried Tom. "Drop it down, Ned! Drop it down! We're going to be right over the tree in another second or two!"

Ned leaned over the side of the craft and had a good view of the strange sight. The tree that was on fire was a dead oak of great size, dwarfing the other trees in the grove in which it stood. In common with other oaks this one still retained many of its dried leaves, though it was devoid, or almost devoid, of life. Ned noticed in the branches many irregularly shaped objects, and it appeared to be these that were on fire, blazing fiercely.

"It looks as though some one had tied bundles of sticks in the tree and set them on fire," Ned thought as he poised the opened tin of the evil-smelling compound on the edge of the aeroplane's cockpit.

"Let her go, Ned!" cried Tom. "You'll be too late in another second!"

Ned raised himself in his seat and threw, rather than let fall, the can straight for the blazing tree. Like a bomb it shot toward earth, and Ned and Tom, looking down, could see it strike a limb and break open, the rupture of the can letting loose the liquid contained in it.

And then, before the eyes of Tom and Ned, the

fire seemed to die out as a picture melts away on a moving picture screen. The smoke rolled away in a ball-like cloud, and the flames ceased to crackle and roar.

"Well, for the love of molasses! what happened, Tom?" cried Ned, as the young inventor guided his craft about in a big circle to come back again over the tree. He wanted to make sure that the fire was out.

It was!

"What sent that blaze to the happy hunting grounds?" asked Ned.

"My new aerial extinguisher," answered Tom, with justifiable pride in his voice. "This fire happened in the nick of time for me, Ned. I had a tin of my new combination in the car, not with any intention of using it, though. I intended to pour it in the new containers I am having made in Newmarket to see if it would corrode them, a thing I wish to avoid.

"But when I saw that tree on fire I couldn't resist the temptation to use my very latest combination of chemicals. It is so recent that I haven't actually tried it on a blaze yet, though I had figured out in theory that it ought to work. And it did, Ned! It worked!"

"Well, I should say so!" agreed his chum. "That blaze was doused for fair. The test could not have been better. But what in the name of a volunteer fire department set that tree to blazing, Tom?"

"I'll tell you in a moment. I want to make some notes before I forget. That combination seems to be just of the right strength. It did the trick. Here, take the wheel and hold her steady while I jot down some memoranda before they get away from me."

Ned was capable of managing an airship, especially under Tom's watchful eye, and as this craft was one with dual controls there was no difficulty in shifting from one steersman to the other.

So while Ned guided, now and then gazing down at the tree from which some smoke still arose, though the fire was all out, Tom made the necessary scientific notes for future amplification.

"And now," observed Ned, as his chum resumed the wheel, "suppose you enlighten me on how that tree came to be on fire—if you didn't set it yourself."

"No, I didn't do that," Tom said, with a laugh. "And I only have a theory as to the cause of the blaze. But suppose we go down and take a look. There's a good field around this grove, and we can get a fine take off. I'll have to go back to

Shopton anyhow, to get some more of the chemical."

So the aeroplane made a landing, and then the mystery was explained. The dead oak, to which some of its last year's foliage still clung, was the abiding place of thousands of crows that had built their nests in it. There were hundreds of the big nests, made of dried sticks, mostly, and these made an ideal fuel for the fire.

"But where are the crows, and what started the fire?" asked Ned.

"I fancy the birds flew away as soon as they saw their homes on fire," said Tom. "Or they may not have been at home. Flocks of crows often go to some distant feeding ground for the day, returning at night. I fancy that is what happened here.

"As for the cause of the blaze, I believe it was set by some mischievous boys, who saw a good chance to have some fun without thought of doing any real damage. For the dead tree was of no value, and I imagine the farmers would be glad to see the flock of crows dispersed. Some boys probably climbed up and set fire to one of the nests, and then, when they saw the whole lot going, they became frightened and ran away."

And Tom's theory was, eventually, proved to be

true. Some lads, wandering afield, had set fire to the crows' nests and then, frightened as they saw a bigger blaze than they intended, ran away.

Tom and Ned did not remain to see what the returning crows might think about the destruction of their homes, provided they saw fit to return, but, starting the aeroplane, were again on their way.

Tom had lingered long enough to make sure that his latest combination of chemicals had been just what was needed. He felt sure that by using a larger quantity, no fire, however fierce, could continue to blaze.

"But I want to give it a good trial, Ned, as we did from the tower," said Tom. "Though I don't believe there'll be a fizzle this time."

It did not take long for Tom to secure another supply of the new chemical. He then went with it to the firm in Newmarket that was making his containers, or "bombs" as he called them.

On his return he consulted with Mr. Baxter as to the ingredients of the fluid that had put out the blaze in the tree.

"I believe you have at last hit on the right combination," said the chemist. "You are on the road to success, Tom. I wish I could say the same of myself."

"Perhaps your formulæ may come back to you

as suddenly as they disappeared, or as quickly as I discovered that I had the right thing to put out the fire," said Tom hopefully.

Busy days followed for the young inventor. Now that he was convinced he had at last evolved the right mixture of chemicals, he prepared to make a test on a larger scale than merely a blazing tree.

"I'll try it with a fire in the pit," he said to his chum.

Preparations were made, and the day before Tom was to carry out his plans he received a letter.

"What's the matter? Bad news?" asked Ned, as he saw his friend's face change after reading the epistle.

"Nothing much. Only Mary is going away, and I had expected her to be at the test," Tom answered.

"Going away?" echoed Ned. "For long?"

"Oh, no, only for a couple of weeks. She is going to visit an uncle and aunt in Newmarket, or just outside of that city. Another uncle, Barton Keith, has offices in the Landmark Building, I believe."

"Landmark Building," murmured Ned. "Isn't that where Field and Melling hang out?"

"Yes. But don't mention Mary's uncle in connection with them," laughed Tom. "He wouldn't like it."

"I should say not!"

Ned well remembered Mary's uncle, who had been associated with Tom in recovering the treasure in the undersea search.

"Well, if she can't be here, she can't," said Tom, as philosophically as possible. "I'd better run over and bid her good-bye."

This Tom did, though Ned noticed that his chum acted as though lonesome on his return.

"But when he gets to work testing his new chemical he'll be all right," decided Ned.

CHAPTER XIII

A SUCCESSFUL TEST

"IT took you long enough," Ned remarked as Tom entered the main office of the plant, having been to see Mary off on her trip to Newmarket. This was following his call of the night before to learn more particulars of her unexpected visit.

"Yes, I didn't plan to be gone so long," apologized Tom. "But I thought while I was there I might as well go all the way with her."

"And did you?"

"Yes. In the electric runabout. I wanted to come back and get the airship, but she said she wanted to look nice when she met her relatives, and as yet airship travel is a bit mussy. Though when I get my cabined cruiser of the clouds I'll guarantee not to ruffle a curl of the daintiest girl!"

"Getting poetical in your old age!" laughed Ned. "Well, here is that statement you said you wanted me to get ready. Want to go over it now?"

"No, I guess not, as long as you know it's all

right. I'm going to start right in and get ready for a bang-up test."

"Of what—your new aerial fire fighting apparatus?"

"Yes. Mr. Baxter and I are going to make up a lot of the chemical compound that—we discovered through using it on the blazing tree—will best do the trick. Then I'm going to try it on a pit fire, and after that on a big blaze with an airship."

"Let me know when you do," begged Ned. "I want to see you do it."

"I'll send you word," promised the young inventor.

Then he began several days and nights of hard work. And he was glad to have the chance to occupy himself, for, though Tom professed not to be much affected by the departure of Mary Nestor, he really was very lonesome.

"How is her uncle, Barton Keith, by the way?" asked Ned, when he called on his chum one day, to find him reading a letter which needed but half an eye to tell was from Mary.

"About as usual," was the answer. "He sends word by Mary that he'll be glad to see us any time we want to call. He has some nice offices in the Landmark Building."

"Those papers proving his right to the oil land,

which you recovered from the sunken ship for him, must have made his fortune."

"Well, yes—that and other things," agreed Tom. "Say, we had some exciting times on that undersea search, didn't we?"

"Did you call on Mr. Keith when you went to Newmarket with Mary?" Ned wanted to know, for he and Tom had taken quite a liking to Miss Nestor's uncle.

"No, I didn't get a chance. Besides, I wanted to keep away from the Landmark Building."

"Why?"

"Oh, I might run into Field and Melling, and I don't want to see them until I can accuse them, and prove it, of having taken Mr. Baxter's dye formulæ."

"Oh, yes, they're in the same building with Mr. Keith, aren't they? Why do they call it the Landmark? Though I suppose the answer is obvious."

"Yes," assented Tom. "It's a big building— the tallest ever erected in that city, and a fine structure. Though while they were about it I don't see why they didn't make it fireproof."

"Didn't they?" asked Ned, in surprise. "Then the insurance rates must be unusually high, for the companies are beginning to realize how fire departments, even in big cities, are hampered in fighting blazes above the tenth or twelfth stories."

"Yes, it was a mistake not to have the Land-mark Building fireproof," admitted Tom. "And Mr. Keith says the owners are beginning to realize that now. It is what is called the 'slow burning' construction."

"Insurance companies don't go much on that," declared Ned, who was in a position to know. "Well, let us hope it never catches fire."

These were busy days for the young inventor. He laid aside all his other activities in order to perfect the plans for manufacturing his new chemical fire extinguisher on a large scale. For Tom realized that while a small quantity of chemicals in a compound might act in a certain way on one occasion, if the bulk should happen to be increased the experimenter could not always count on invariably the same results.

There appeared to be at times a change en-gendered when a large quantity of chemicals were mixed which was not manifest in a small and ex-perimental batch.

So Tom wanted to mix up a big tank of his new chemical compound and see if it would work in large quantities as well as it did with the small amount Ned had dropped on the blazing tree.

To this end Tom worked at night, as well as by day, and finally he announced to Ned and Mr.

Damon, who called one evening, that he believed he had everything in readiness for an exhaustive test the next day.

"There's the stuff!" exclaimed Tom, not a little proudly, as he waved his hand toward an immense carboy in the main shop. "That's what I hope will do the trick. Just take a——"

"Hold on! Stop! That's enough! Bless my hair brush!" cried Mr. Damon, holding up a protesting hand. "If you take that cork out, Tom Swift, you and I will cease to be friends!"

"I wasn't going to open it," laughed the young inventor. "It has a worse odor and seems to choke you more in a big quantity than when there's only a little. I was just going to shake the carboy to let you realize how full it was."

"We'll take your word for it!" laughed Ned. "Now about your test. How are you going to work it?"

"There are to be two tests," answered Tom. "The first, and the smaller, will be in the pit, as before, only this time we shall have what, I believe, will be the successful combination of chemicals to drop on it.

"The second test will be the main one. In that I plan to have an old barn which I have bought set ablaze. Then Ned and I will sail over it in the airship and drop chemicals on it. The barn will be filled with empty boxes and barrels, to make as hot a fire as possible. You are invited to accompany us, Mr. Damon."

"Will there be any smell?" asked the eccentric man, who seemed to have a dislike for anything that was not as agreeable as perfume.

"No, the chemicals will be sealed in containers, which will be dropped from my airship as bombs were dropped in the war," said Tom.

"On those conditions I'll go along," agreed Mr. Damon. "But bless my wedding certificate, Tom! don't tell my wife. She thinks I'm crazy enough now, associating with you and flying occasionally. If she thought I would help you battle with flames from the air she'd likely never speak to me again."

"I'll not tell," promised Tom, laughing.

Preparations for the test went on rapidly. In the morning a fire was to be started in the same pit where the experiment had partly failed before.

From the platform over the blazing hole some of the new combination of chemicals was to be dropped. If it acted with success, as Tom believed it would, he proposed to go on with the more important test in the afternoon.

To this end he had purchased from a farmer the right to set on fire an old ramshackle barn, standing in the midst of a field about three miles outside of Shopton. The barn was on an untilled farm, the house having been destroyed some years before, and it was not near any other structures, so that, even in a high wind, no damage would result.

Tom had filled the barn with inflammable material, and was going to spare no effort to have the test as exhaustive as possible.

The time came for the preliminary trial, and there were a few anxious moments after the oil-soaked boards and boxes in the pit were set ablaze.

"Let her go!" cried Tom to his man on the elevated platform, and down fell the container of chemicals. It had no sooner struck and burst, letting loose a mass of flame-choking vapor, than the fire died out.

"You've struck it, Tom! You've struck it!" cried Ned.

"It begins to look so," agreed the young inventor. "But I'll not call myself out of the woods until this afternoon. Though we can consider it a success so far."

Quite a throng was on hand when the old barn was set ablaze. Tom and Ned and Mr. Damon were there with the airship which had been especially fitted to carry the bombs filled with the extinguisher.

In order to insure a quick, hot blaze the barn was fired on all four sides at once by Tom's men. When it was seen to be a veritable raging furnace of fire, Tom and his two friends took their places in the airship and rapidly mounted upward.

Necessarily they had to circle off away from the blaze to get to the necessary height, but Tom soon brought the airship around again and headed for the black pall of smoke which marked the place of the blazing barn.

"We'll all three send down bombs at the same time," Tom told his friends, as they darted forward. "When I give the word press the levers, and the chemical containers will drop. Then we'll hope for the best."

Higher mounted the flames, and more fiercely raged the fire. The heat of it penetrated even aloft, where Tom and his friends were scudding along in the airship.

"Now!" cried Tom, as his craft hovered for an instant in a favorable position for dropping the bombs. The young inventor, Mr. Damon, and Ned Newton pressed the levers. Looking over the sides of the craft, they saw three dark objects dropping into the midst of the burning barn.

CHAPTER XIV

OUT OF THE CLOUDS

ALMOST as though some giant hand had dropped an immense cloak over the fire in the barn, so did the blaze die down instantly after Tom Swift's extinguishing liquid had been dropped into the seething caldron of flame. For a moment there was even no smoke, but as the embers remained hot and glowing for a time, though the flames themselves were quenched, a rolling vapor cloud began to ascend shortly after the first cessation of the fire. But this only lasted a little while.

"You've turned the trick, Tom!" cried Ned, leaning far over to look at what was left of the barn and its contents.

"Bless my insurance policy, I should say so!" exclaimed Mr. Damon. "It was certainly neat work, Tom!"

"It does look as if I'd struck the right combination," admitted Tom, and he felt justifiable pride in his achievement.

"Look so! Why, hang it all, man, it *is* so!" declared Ned. "That fire went out as if sent for by a special delivery telegram to give a hurry-up performance in another locality. Look, there's hardly any smoke even!"

This was so, as the three occupants of the rapidly moving airship could see when Tom circled back to pass again over the almost destroyed structure. He had waited until it was almost consumed before dropping his chemicals, as he wished to make the test hard and conclusive. Now the fire was out except for a few small spots spouting up here and there, away from the center of the blaze.

"Yes, I guess she doesn't need a second dose," observed Tom, when he saw how effective had been his treatment of the fire. "I had an additional batch of chemicals on hand, in case they were needed," he added, and he tapped some unused bombs at his feet.

"I call this a pretty satisfactory test," declared Ned. "If you want to form a stock company, Tom, and put your aerial fire-fighting apparatus on the market, I'll guarantee to underwrite the securities."

"Hardly that yet," said Tom, with a laugh. "Now that I have my chemical combination perfected, or practically so, I've got to rig up an airship that will be especially adapted for fighting fires in sky-scrapers."

"What more do you want than this?" asked Ned, as his chum prepared to descend in the speedy machine.

"I want a little better bomb-releasing device, for one thing. This worked all right. But I want one that is more nearly automatic. Then I am going to put on a searchlight, so I can see where I am heading at night."

"Not your great big one!" cried Ned, recalling the immense electric lantern that had so aided in capturing the Canadian smugglers.

"No. But one patterned after that." Tom answered.

"Bless my candlestick!" exclaimed Mr. Damon, "what do you want with a searchlight at a fire, Tom? Isn't there light enough at a blaze, anyhow?"

"No," answered the young inventor, as he made his usual skillful landing. "You know all the big city fire departments have searchlights now for night work and where there is thick smoke. It may be that same day, in fighting a sky-scraper blaze from the clouds at night, I'll have need of more illumination than comes from the flames themselves."

"Well, you ought to know. You've made a

study of it," said Mr. Damon, as he and Ned alighted with Tom, the latter receiving congratulations from a number of his friends, including members of the Shopton fire department who were present to witness the test.

"Mighty clever piece of work, Tom Swift!" declared a deputy chief. "Of course we won't have much use for any such apparatus here in Shopton, as we haven't any big buildings. But in New York, Chicago, Pittsburg and other cities —why, it will be just what they need, to my way of thinking."

"And he needn't go so far from home," said Mr. Damon. "There is one tall building over in Newmarket—the Landmark. I happen to own a little stock in the corporation that put that up, along with other buildings, and I'm going to have them adopt Tom Swift's aerial fire-fighting apparatus."

"Thank you. But you don't need to go to that trouble," asserted Tom. "My idea isn't to have every sky-scraper equipped with an airship extinguisher."

"No? What then?" asked Mr. Damon.

"Well, I think there ought to be one, or perhaps two, in a big city like New York," Tom answered. "Perhaps one outfit would be enough, for it isn't likely that there would be two big fires in the tall building section at the same time, and an airship could easily cover the distance between two widely separated blazes. But if I can perfect this machine so it will be available for fires out of the reach of apparatus on the ground, I'll be satisfied."

"You'll do it, Tom, don't worry about that!" declared the deputy chief. "I never saw a slicker piece of work than this!"

And that was the verdict of all who had witnessed the performance.

With the successful completion of this exacting test and the knowledge that he had perfected the major part of his aerial fire-extinguisher—the chemical combination—Tom Swift was now able to devote his attention to the "frills" as Ned called them. That is, he could work out a scheme for attaching a searchlight to his airship and make better arrangements for a one-man control in releasing the chemical containers into the heart of a big blaze.

Tom Swift owned several airships, and he finally selected one of not too great size, but very powerful, that would hold three and, if necessary, four persons. This was rebuilt to enable a considerable quantity of the fire-extinguishing liquid to be stored in the under part of the somewhat limited cockpit.

This much done, and while his men were making up a quantity of the extinguisher, using the secret formula, and storing it in suitable containers, Tom began attaching a searchlight to his "cloud fire-engine," as Koku called it.

The giant was aching to be with Tom and help in the new work, but Koku was faithful to the blinded Eradicate, and remained almost constantly with the old colored man.

It was touching to see the two together, the giant trying, in his kind, but imperfect way, to anticipate the wishes of the other, with whom he had so often disputed and quarreled in days past. Now all that was forgotten, and Koku gave up being with Tom to wait on Eradicate.

While the colored man was, in fact, unable to see, following the accident when Tom was experimenting with the fire extinguisher, it was hoped that sight might be restored to one eye after an operation. This operation had to be postponed until the eyes and wounds in the face were sufficiently healed.

Meanwhile Rad suffered as patiently as possible, and Koku shared his loneliness in the sick room. Tom came to see Rad as often as he could, and did everything possible to make his aged servant's lot happier. But Rad wanted to be up and about, and it was pathetic to hear him ask about the little tasks he had been wont to perform in the past.

Rad was delighted to hear of Tom's success with the new apparatus, after having been told how quickly the barn fire was put out.

"Yo'—yo' jest wait twell I gits up, Massa Tom," said Rad. "Den Ah'll help make all de contraptions on de airship."

"All right, Rad, there'll be plenty for you to do when the time comes," said the inventor. And he could not help a feeling of sadness as he left the colored man's room.

"I wonder if he is doomed to be blind the rest of his life," thought Tom. "I hope not, for if he does it will be my fault for letting him try to mix those chemicals."

But, hoping for the best, Tom plunged into the work ahead of him. He did not want to offer his aerial fire extinguisher to any large city until he had perfected it, and he was now laboring to that end.

One day, in midsummer, after weary days of toil, Tom took Ned out for a ride in the machine which had been fitted up to carry a large supply of the chemical mixture, a small but powerful searchlight, and other new "wrinkles" as Tom called them, not going into details.

"Any special object in view?" asked Ned, as

Tom headed across country. "Are you going to put out any more tree fires?"

"No, I haven't that in mind," was the answer. "Though of course if we come across a blaze, except a brush fire, I may put it out. I have the bombs here," and Tom indicated the releasing lever.

"What I want to try now is the stability of this with all I have on board," he resumed. "If she is able to travel along, and behave as well as she did before I made the changes, I'll know she is going to be all right. I don't expect to put out any fires this trip."

In testing the ship of the air Tom sent her up to a good height, heading out over the open country and toward a lake on the shores of which were a number of summer resorts. It was now the middle of the season, and many campers, cottagers and hotel folk were scattered about the wooded shore of the pretty and attractive body of water.

Tom and Ned had a glimpse of the lake, dotted with many motor boats and other craft, as the airship ascended until it was above the clouds. Then, for a time, nothing could be seen by the occupants but masses of feathery vapor.

"She's working all right," decided Tom, when he found that he could perform his usual aerial feats with his craft, laden as she was with apparatus, as well as he had been able to do before she was so burdened. "Guess we might as well go down, Ned. There isn't much more to do, as far as I can see."

Down out of the heights they swept at a rapid pace. A few moments later they had burst through the film of clouds and once more the lake was below them in clear view.

Suddenly Ned pointed to something on the water and cried:

"Look, Tom! Look! A motor boat in some kind of trouble! She's sinking!"

CHAPTER XV

COALS OF FIRE

Tom Swift saw the craft almost as soon as did his chum. It was rather a large-sized motor boat, quite some distance out from shore, and there was no other craft near it at this time. From the quick, first view Tom and Ned had of it, they decided that a party of excursionists were on a pleasure trip.

But that an accident had happened, and that trouble, if not, indeed, danger, was imminent, was at once apparent to the young inventor and the other occupant of the swiftly moving airship.

For as Tom shut off his motor, to volplane down, thus reducing all noise on his craft, they could dimly hear the shouts and calls for help, coming from the water craft below them.

"Help! Help!" came the impassioned appeals, floating up to Tom and Ned.

"We're coming!" Tom answered, though it is doubtful if his voice was heard. Sound does not seem to carry downward as well as upward, and though Tom's craft was making scarcely any noise, save that caused by the rush of wind through the struts and wires, there was so much confusion on the motor boat, to say nothing of the engine which was going, that Tom's encouraging call must have been unheard.

"What are you going to do, Tom?" asked Ned. "You can't land on the water!"

"I know it; worse luck! If I only had the hydroplane, now, we could make a thrilling rescue—land right beside the other boat and take 'em all off. But, as it is, I'll have to land as near as I can and then we will look for a boat to go out to them in."

Ned saw, now, what Tom's object was. On one shore of the lake was a large, level field, suitable for a landing place for the craft of the air. At least it looked to be a suitable place, but Tom would be obliged to take a chance on that. This field sloped down to the beach of the lake, and as Ned and his chum came nearer to earth they could see several boats on shore, though no persons were near them. Had there been, probably they would have gone to the rescue.

Tom cast a rapid look across the sheet of water, to make sure his services were really needed. The motor boat was lower in the lake now, and was, undoubtedly, sinking. And no other craft was near enough to render help. Though distant whistles, seeming to come from approaching craft, told of help on the way.

"Hold fast, Ned!" cried Tom, as they neared the earth. "We may bump!"

But Tom Swift was too skillful a pilot to cause his craft to sustain much of a crash. He made an almost perfect "three point landing," and there would have been no unusual shaking, except for the fact that the field was a bit bumpy, and the craft more heavily laden than usual.

"Good work, Tom!" cried Ned, as the *Lucifer* slackened her speed, the young inventor having sent her around in a half circle so that she now faced the lake. Then Tom and Ned climbed from the cockpit, throwing off goggles and helmets as they ran to the shore where there were several rowboats moored.

"And a little old-fashioned naphtha launch! By all that's lucky!" cried Tom. "I didn't think they made these any more. If she only works now!"

There was a little dock at this point on the lake, and the boats appeared to be held at it for hire. But no one was in charge, and Tom and Ned made free with what they found. They considered they had this right in the emergency.

The naphtha launch was chained and padlocked

to the dock, but using an oar Tom burst the chain.

"Get one of the rowboats and fasten it to the back of the launch!" Tom directed Ned. "I don't believe this craft will hold them all," and he nodded toward those aboard the sinking boat —for it was only too plainly sinking now.

"All right!" voiced Ned. "I'm with you. Can you get that engine to work?"

"She's humming now," announced Tom, as he turned on the naphtha, and threw in a blazing match to ignite it, this act saving his hand. Naphtha engines are a trifle treacherous.

A few moments later, though not as quickly as a gasoline craft could have been gotten under way, Tom was steering the small launch out and away from the dock, and toward the craft whence came the faint calls for help. Behind them Tom and Ned towed a large rowboat.

Tom speeded the naphtha craft to its limit, and, fortunately for those in danger, it was a fast boat. In less time than they had thought possible, the young inventor and his chum were near the boat that was now low in the water—so low, in fact, that her rail was all but awash.

"Oh, take us out! Save us!" screamed some of the girls.

"Take it easy now," advised Tom, approaching with care. "We've got room for you all. Ned, get back in the rowboat and bring that alongside—on the other side. We'll take you all in," he added.

"Girls first!" called Ned sternly, as he saw one young fellow about to scramble into the naphtha boat.

"Sure, girls first!" agreed the skipper of the disabled craft. "Hit a submerged log," he explained to Tom, as the work of rescue proceeded. "Stove a hole in the bow, but we stuffed coats and things in, and made it a slow leak. Kept the engine going as long as we could, but I thought no one would ever come! Lucky you happened to see us from up there!"

"Yes," assented Tom shortly. He and Ned were too busy to talk much, as they were aiding in getting some hysterical girls and young women into the two sound craft. And when the last of the picnic party had been taken off, the boat with a hole in it gave a sudden lurch, there was a gurgling, bubbling sound, and she sank quickly.

Tom and Ned had anticipated this, however, and had their craft well out of the way of the suction.

"You'll all have to sit quiet," Tom warned his passengers as he took Ned's boat, with her load, in tow. "I've got about all the law allows me to carry," he added grimly.

"Oh, what ever would we have done without you?" half sobbed one girl.

"I guess you could have managed to swim ashore," Tom answered, not wanting to make too much of his effort.

Then more rescue boats came up, but those in the naphtha craft, and Ned's smaller one, refused to be transferred, and remained with our friends until safely landed at the dock.

Receiving the half-hysterical thanks of the party, and leaving them to explain matters to the owner of the borrowed boats, Ned and Tom went back to the *Lucifer,* and were soon aloft again.

"Pretty slick act, Tom," remarked Ned.

"Oh, it's all in the day's work," was the answer.

He had all but perfected his big fire-extinguishing aeroplane, and was contemplating means by which he could give a demonstration to the fire department of some big city, when Mr. Baxter asked to see Tom one day. There was a look on the face of the chemist that caused Tom to exclaim with a good deal of concern:

"What's the matter?"

"Only the same old trouble," was the discouraged answer. "I can't get on the track of my lost secret formulæ. If I had Field and Melling here now I—I'd——"

He did not finish his threat, but the look on his face was enough to show his righteous anger.

"I wish we could do something to those fellows!" exclaimed Tom energetically. "If we only had some direct evidence against them!"

"I've got evidence enough—in my own mind!" declared Mr. Baxter.

"Unfortunately that doesn't do in law," returned Tom. "But now that I have this airship fire-fighter craft so nearly finished, I can devote more time to your troubles, Mr. Baxter."

"Oh, I don't want you bothered over my troubles," said the chemist. "You have enough of your own. But I'm at my wit's end what to do next."

"If it is money matters," began Tom.

"It's partly that, yes," said the other, in a low voice. "If I had those dye formulæ, I'd be a rich man."

"Well, let me help you temporarily," begged Tom. And the upshot of the talk was that he engaged Mr. Baxter to do certain research work in the Swift laboratories until such time as the chemist could perfect certain other inventions on which he was working.

In return for his kindness to a fellow laborer,

Tom received from Mr. Baxter some valuable
hints about fire-extinguishing chemicals, one hint,
alone, serving to bring about a curious situation.

It was several days after the accident to the
motor boat from which the young inventor and
Ned Newton had rescued the party of pleasure
seekers that Tom was visited by Mr. Damon,
who drove over in his car.

"Have you anything special to do, Tom?" asked
the eccentric man. "If you haven't I wish you'd
take a ride with me. Not for mere pleasure!
Bless my excursion ticket, don't think that, Tom!"
cried his friend quickly.

"I know better than to ask you out for a
pleasure jaunt. But I have become interested in
a certain candy-making machine that a man over
in Newmarket is anxious to sell me a share in,
and I'd like to get your opinion. Can you run
over?"

"Yes," Tom answered. "As it happens I am
going to Newmarket myself."

"Oh, I forgot about Mary Nestor being there!"
laughed Mr. Damon. "Sly dog, Tom! Sly
dog!" and he nudged the youth in the ribs.

"It isn't altogether Mary. Though I am going
to see her," Tom admitted. "It has to do with a
little apparatus I am getting up. I can capture
several birds in the same auto, so I'll go along."

This pleased Mr. Damon, and he and Tom were soon speeding over the road. It was just outside Newmarket that they saw an automobile stalled at the foot of a hill which they topped. It needed but a glance to show that there was serious trouble. As Mr. Damon's car went down the slope two men could be seen leaping from the other machine. And, as they did so, flames burst out of the rear of the stalled machine.

"Fire! Fire!" cried Mr. Damon, rather needlessly it would seem, as any one could see the blaze.

"Another chance!" exclaimed Tom, reaching down between his feet for a wrapped object he had placed in Mr. Damon's car. "It's Field and Melling!" he cried. "The two men who boasted of having put it over on Mr. Baxter. Their car is blazing. Here's where I get a chance to heap coals of fire on their heads!"

CHAPTER XVI

VIOLENT THREATS

Tom Swift's companion in the automobile was sufficiently acquainted with this old expression to understand readily what it meant. And as he directed his car as close as was safe to the blazing car, Mr. Damon asked:

"Are you going to put out that fire for them, Tom?"

"I'm going to try," was the grim answer.

The young inventor was rapidly taking out of wrapping paper a metal cylinder with a short nozzle on one end and a handle on the other. It was, obviously, a hand fire extinguisher of a type familiar to all.

"Wait Tom, I'll slow up a little more," said Mr. Damon, as he applied the brakes with more force. "Bless my court plaster! don't jump and injure yourself."

But Tom Swift was sufficiently agile to leap from the automobile when it was still making good speed. He did not want Mr. Damon to approach too close to the burning car, for there might be an explosion. At the same time, he rather discounted the risk to himself, for he ran right in, while the two men, who had leaped from the blazing machine, hurried to a safe distance.

Tom held in readiness a small hand extinguisher. It was one he had constructed from an old one found in the shop, but it contained some of his own chemicals, the original solution having been used at some time or other. It was the intention of the young inventor to put on the market a house-size extinguisher after he had disposed of his big airship invention.

"Look out there! The gasoline tank may go up!" cried Field, the small man with the big voice.

Tom did not answer, but ran in as close as was necessary and began to play a small stream from his hand extinguisher on the blazing car. He was thus able to direct the white, frothy chemical better than when he had shot it from the airship, and in a few seconds only some wisps of curling smoke remained to tell of the presence of the fire. The automobile was badly charred, but the damage was not past redemption.

"Bless my check book! you did the trick, Tom," cried Mr. Damon, as he alighted and came up to congratulate his companion.

"Yes. But this wasn't much," Tom said. "I

didn't use half the charge. Short circuit?" he asked Field and Melling who were now returning, having seen that the danger was passed.

"I—I guess so," replied Melling, in his squeaky voice. "We—we are much obliged to you."

"No thanks necessary," said Tom, a bit shortly, as he turned to go back with Mr. Damon to their car. "It's what any one would do under like circumstances."

"Only you did it very effectively," observed Field.

Tom was wondering if they knew who he was and of his association with Josephus Baxter. He did not believe the men recognized him as the person who had been at the Meadow Inn one day with Mary. They had hardly glanced at him then, he thought.

"That's a mighty powerful extinguisher you have there, young man," said Melling. "May I ask the make of it? We ought to carry one like it on our car," he told his companion.

"It is the Swift Aerial Fire Extinguisher," said Tom gravely, with a glance at Mr. Damon.

"The Swift—*Tom* Swift?" exclaimed Melling. "Do you mean——"

"I am Tom Swift," put in the young inventor quickly. "And this is one of my inventions. I might add," he said slowly, looking first Melling and then Field full in the face, "that I was aided in perfecting the chemical extinguisher by Josephus Baxter."

The effect on the two men, whom Tom believed were scoundrels, was marked.

"Baxter!" cried Field.

"Is *he* associated with you?" demanded Melling.

"Not officially," Tom answered, delighted at the chance to "rub it in," as he expressed it later. "I have been helping him, and he has been helping me since he lost his dye formulæ in—in your fire!"

"Does he say he lost them in the fire of our factory?" demanded Field aggressively.

"He believes he did," asserted Tom. "I helped carry him out of the laboratory of your place when he was almost dead from suffocation. He remembers that he had the formulæ then, but since has been unable to find them."

"He'd better be careful how he accuses us!" blustered Field, in his big voice.

"We could have the law on him for that!" squeaked the bigger Melling.

"He hasn't accused you," said Tom easily. "He only says the formulæ disappeared during the fire in your place, and he is just wondering, that is all—just *wondering!*"

"Well, he—we, I—that is, we haven't anything from Baxter that we didn't pay for," declared Field. "And if he goes about saying such things he'd better be careful. I am going——"

But he suddenly became silent as his companion's elbow nudged him. And then Melling took up the talk, saying:

"We're much obliged to you, Mr. Swift, for putting out the fire in our car. But for you it would have been destroyed. And if you ever want to sell the extinguisher process of yours, you'll find us in the market. We are going into the dye business on a large scale, and we can always use new chemical combinations."

"My extinguisher is not for sale," said Tom dryly. "Come on, Mr. Damon. We can take you into town, I suppose," Tom went on, looking at his eccentric friend for confirmation, and finding it in a nod. "But I doubt if we could tow you, as we are in a hurry, and——"

"Oh, thank you, we'll look over our machine before we leave it," said Melling. "It may be that we can get it to go."

Tom doubted this, after a look at the charred section, but he easily understood the dislike of the men, upon whose heads he had heaped coals of fire, to ride with him and Mr. Damon.

So Field and Melling were left standing in the

road near their stranded car, which, but for Tom Swift's prompt action, would have been only a heap of ruins.

Tom first visited the man who had a candy machine, in which the owner wanted to interest Mr. Damon. After seeing a demonstration and giving his opinion, he attended to his own affairs, in which his hand extinguisher played a part. Then he called on Mary Nestor at her relative's home.

"Oh, but it's good to see you again, Tom!" cried Mary, after the first greeting. "What have you been doing, and what's all that white stuff on your coat?"

"Fire extinguisher chemical," Tom answered, and he related what had happened.

"What's the matter with your aunt, Mary? She seems worried about something," he said, after the aunt with whom Mary was staying had come in, greeted Tom briefly, and gone out again.

"Oh, she and Uncle Jasper are worried over money matters, I believe," Mary said. "Uncle Jasper invested heavily in the Landmark Building here, and now, I understand, it is discovered that it was put up in violation of the building laws—something about not being fire-proof. Uncle Jasper is likely to lose considerable money.

"It isn't that it will make him so very poor,"

Mary went on. "But Uncle Barton Keith—you remember you went on the undersea search with him—Uncle Barton warned Uncle Jasper not to go into the Landmark Building scheme."

"And Uncle Jasper did, I take it," said Tom.

"Yes. And now he's sorry, for not only may he lose money, but Uncle Barton will laugh at him, and Uncle Jasper hates that worse than losing a lot. But tell me about yourself, Tom. What have you been doing? And is Eradicate going to get better?"

"I hope so," Tom said. "As for me——"

But he was interrupted by loud voices in the hall. He recognized the tones of Mary's Uncle Jasper saying:

"They're scoundrels, that's what they are! Just plain scoundrels! When I accuse them of swindling me and others in that Landmark Building deal they have the nerve to ask me to invest money in some secret dye formulæ they claim will revolutionize the industry! Bah! They're scoundrels, that's what they are—Field and Melling are scoundrels, and I'm going to have them arrested!"

CHAPTER XVII

A TOWN BLAZE

MARY'S uncle, Jasper Blake, always an impetuous man, opened the door so quickly that Tom, who was standing near it talking to Mary, barely had time to move aside.

"Oh, Tom, excuse me! Didn't see you!" bruskly went on Mr. Blake. "But this thing has gotten on my nerves and I guess I'm a bit wrought up."

"There isn't any guessing about it, Uncle Jasper," said Mary, with a laugh and a look at Tom to warn him not to tell her relative that he had just befriended Field and Melling. "For," as Mary said to Tom later, "he would positively rave at you."

Tom was wise enough to realize this, and so, after some laughing reference to the effect that he would have to wear protective armor if he stood near doors when Mary's uncle opened them so suddenly, the conversation became general.

"I hope you never get roped in as I have been," said Mr. Blake, as he sat down. "Those

scoundrels, Field and Melling, would rob a baby
of his first tooth if they had the chance!"

"No, I am not likely to have anything to do
with them; though I have met them," and Tom
gave Mary a glance. "But did I hear you say
they are embarking on a dye enterprise?" he
asked. "I couldn't help overhearing what you
said in the hall," he explained.

"That's the story they tell," said Uncle Jasper.
"I was foolish enough to invest in the Landmark
Building, and now I'm likely to lose it all in a
lawsuit."

"I mentioned it," said Mary.

"And that isn't the worst," went on Mr. Blake.
"But Barton—that's your friend of the submarine
—will give me the laugh, for he was asked to invest in the same building, and didn't."

"Oh, maybe it will all turn out right," said Tom
consolingly. "My friend Mr. Damon has a little
stock in the same structure."

"Nothing those two scoundrels have anything
to do with will turn out right," declared Mary's
uncle. "And to think of their nerve when they
ask me to go in with them on a dye scheme!"

"That's what interests me," said Tom.

"Well, take my advice and don't become interested to the extent of investing any money,"
warned Mr. Blake. "I'm not going to."

"I didn't mean that way," said Tom. "But I happen to be acquainted with an expert dye maker who lost some secret formulæ during a fire in Field and Melling's factory."

"You don't say so!" cried Mr. Blake. "Tom Swift, there's something wrong here! Let you and me talk this over. I begin to see how I may be able to take a peep through the hole in the grindstone," a colloquial expression which was as well understood by Tom as were some of Mr. Damon's blessing remarks.

"If you're going to talk business I think I'll excuse myself," said Mary.

"Don't go," urged Tom, but she said to him that she would see him before he left, and then she went out, leaving her uncle and the young inventor busily engaged in talking.

But though Mr. Blake had certain suspicions regarding Field and Melling, and though Tom Swift, too, believed they had something to do with the disappearance of Baxter's secret formulæ, it was another matter to prove anything.

Impetuous as he often was, Mr. Blake was for calling in the police at once, and having the two men arrested. But Tom counseled delay.

"Wait until we get more evidence against them," he urged.

"But they may skip out!" objected Mary's uncle.

"They won't with that Landmark Building on their hands," said the young inventor.

"*Their* hands! Huh! They'll take precious good care that the trouble and responsibility of it are on other people's hands before they go," declared Mr. Blake. "However, I suppose you're right. Barton Keith sets a deal by your opinion since that undersea search, and while I don't always agree with him, I do in this case. Especially since he is likely to have the laugh on me."

"Oh, I wouldn't count everything lost in that building deal," said Tom. "A way may be found out of the trouble yet. But I must be getting back. Dr. Henderson was to give a report to-day on the condition of Eradicate's eyes, and I want to be there."

"Mary was saying something about your faithful old retainer being in trouble," said Mr. Blake. "I'm sorry to hear about it."

"We are all sorry for poor Rad," replied Tom slowly. "I only hope he gets his sight back. His last days will be very sad if he doesn't."

Tom found Mary waiting for him after he had left her uncle, and, after a short talk with her, he made ready to ride back with Mr. Damon, who, after having attended to several other matters, was now outside in his car.

"When are you coming home, Mary?" Tom asked.

"In a week or two," she answered. "I'll send word when I'm ready and you can come and get me."

"Delighted!" declared Tom. "Don't forget!"

During the ride home the young inventor was unusually silent, so much so that Mr. Damon finally exclaimed:

"Bless my phonograph, Tom Swift! but what is the matter? Has Mary broken the engagement?"

"Oh, no, nothing like that," was the answer. "Only I'm wondering about Eradicate, and— other matters."

Other matters had to do with what Mary's uncle had told Tom about the interest manifested by Field and Melling in some dye industry.

Tom's forebodings regarding his colored helper were nearly borne out, for Dr. Henderson gloomily shook his head when asked for the verdict.

"It's too early to say for a certainty," replied the medical man, "but I am not as hopeful as I was, Tom, I'm sorry to say."

"I'm sorry to hear it," returned Tom. "Is there anything we can do—any hospital to which we can send him for special treatment?"

"No, he is doing as well as he can be expected to right here. Besides, he has his friends around him, and the companionship of that giant of yours, absurd as it may seem, is really a tonic to Eradicate. I never saw such devotion on the part of any one."

"Koku has certainly changed," said Tom. "He and Rad used always to be quarreling. But I guess that is all over," and Tom sighed.

"Oh, I wouldn't say that," declared the medical man. "I haven't given up, though there are some symptoms I do not like. However, I am going to wait a week and then make another test."

Tom knew that the week would be an anxious one for him, but, as it developed, he had so much to do in the next few days that, for the time being, he rather forgot about Eradicate.

Field and Melling, he heard incidentally, had their machine towed to a garage for repairs, but beyond that no word came from the two men. Josephus Baxter remained at work over his dye formulæ in one of Tom's laboratories, but the young inventor did not see much of the discouraged old man.

Tom did not tell of the encounter with Field

and Melling and of extinguishing the fire in their car, for he knew it would only excite Mr. Baxter, and do no good.

It was within a few days of the time when Tom was to call in a committee of fire insurance experts to give them a demonstration of the efficiency of his aerial fire-fighting machine. He was putting the finishing touches to his craft and its extinguishing-dropping devices when he received a call from Mr. Baxter.

"Well, how goes it?" asked Tom, trying to infuse some cheer into his voice.

"Not very well," was the answer. "I've tried, in every way I know, to get on the track of the missing methods perfected by that Frenchman, but I can't. I'd be a millionaire now, if I had that dye information."

"Do you really think they have them—actually have the formulæ?" asked Tom.

"I certainly do. And the reason I believe so is that I was over at a chemical supply factory the other day when an order came in for a quantity of a very rare chemical."

"What has that to do with it?" asked Tom.

"This chemcial is an ingredient called for by one of the dye formulæ that were stolen from me. I never heard of its being used for anything else. I at once became suspicious. I learned that this

chemical had been ordered sent to Field and Melling in their new offices in the Landmark Building."

"Maybe they intend to use it in making a new
kind of fireworks," suggested Tom.

Mr. Baxter shook his head.

"That chemical never would work in a sky-
rocket or Roman candle," he said. "I'm sure
they're trying to cheat me out of my dye formulæ.
If I could only prove it!"

"That's the trouble," agreed Tom. "But I'll
give you all the help I can. And, come to think
of it, I believe you might interest Mr. Blake. He
has no love for Field and Melling, and he has
several keen lawyers on his staff. I believe it
would be a good thing for you to talk to Mr.
Blake."

"Please give me a letter of introduction to
him," begged Mr. Baxter. "What I need is legal
talent and capital to fight these scoundrels. Mr.
Blake may supply both."

"He may," agreed Tom. "I'll fix it so you can
meet him. But what do you think of this combination, Mr. Baxter? It is my very latest solution for putting out fires. I'm loading an airship
up with some of the bomb containers now,
and——"

Tom's further remarks were interrupted by the

noise of shouting and tumult in the street, and a moment later yells could be heard of:

"Fire! Fire! Fire!"

"Another blaze!" exclaimed Mr. Baxter, raising the shades which had been drawn, since night had fallen.

"And not far away," said Tom, as he caught the reflection of a red gleam in the sky.

There was a ring at the front doorbell, and almost at once Ned Newton's voice called:

"Tom! Tom Swift! There's quite a fire in town! Don't you want to try your new apparatus on it?"

"The very chance!" exclaimed the young inventor. "Come on, Mr. Baxter. There's room in the airship for you and Ned. I want you to see how my chemical works!"

Without waiting for a reply from the chemist, Tom caught him by the hand and led him toward the side door that gave egress to the yard where one of the airships was housed. Tom caught sight of Ned, who was hastening toward him.

"Big fire, Tom!" said the young manager again. "Fierce one!"

"I'm going to try to put it out!" Tom answered. "Want to come?"

"Sure thing!" answered Ned.

CHAPTER XVIII

FINISHING TOUCHES

Tom Swift and Ned Newton were so accustomed to acting quickly and in emergencies that it did not take them long to run out the airship, which Tom had in readiness, not especially for this emergency, but to demonstrate his new apparatus to a committee of fire underwriters whom he had invited to call in a few days.

"Take this, if you will, Mr. Baxter!" cried Tom, giving the chemist a metal container. "It's a little different combination from the extinguisher I already have in the machine. Maybe I'll get a chance to try it."

"You're going to have all the chance you want, Tom, by the looks of that blaze," commented Ned Newton.

"It does look like quite a fire," observed Tom, as he gazed up at the sky, where the reflection was turning to a brighter red.

Outside in the streets near the Swift house and shops could be heard the rattle of fire apparatus, the patter of running feet, and many shouts from excited men and boys.

"Any idea what it is, Ned?" asked Tom, as he motioned to Mr. Baxter to climb into the aircraft.

"Some one said it was the new Normal School. But that's farther to the north," was Ned's answer. "By the way the blaze has increased since I first saw it, I'd take it to be the lumber-yard."

"That would make a monster blaze!" observed Tom. "I don't believe I'll have chemicals enough for that," and he looked at the rather small supply in his craft. "However, I haven't time to get any more. Besides, they'll have the regular department on the job, and this isn't a skyscraper, anyhow."

"No, we'll have to go to New York or New-market for one of those," observed Ned. "All ready, Tom?"

"All ready," said the young inventor, as Ned took his place beside Mr. Baxter.

"What's the matter, Tom?" asked the voice of Mr. Swift, as he came out into the yard, having been attracted by the flashing lights and the noise of the aircraft motor, as Tom gave it a pre-liminary test.

"There's a fire in town," Tom answered. "I'm going to see if they need my services."

"Guess there isn't any question about that," said his business manager.

Tom's father, who was suffering the infirmities of age, was in the habit of retiring early, and he had dozed off in his chair directly after supper, to be awakened by the shouting and confusion about the place.

"Take care of yourself, my boy!" he advised, as there came a moment of silence before the throttle of the aircraft was opened to send it on its upward journey. "Don't take too many risks."

"I won't," Tom promised. "We'll be back soon."

Then came the roar of the motor as Tom cut out the muffler to gain speed and, a moment later, he and his two friends were sailing aloft with a load of fire-extinguishing chemicals.

Up and up rose the aircraft. It was not the first time Mr. Baxter had enjoyed the sensation, but he was not enough of a veteran to be immune to the thrills nor to be altogether void of fear. And it was his first night trip. Still he gave few evidences of nervousness.

"There she is!" cried Ned, for when the exhaust from the motor was sent through the new muffler Tom had attached it was possible to talk aboard the *Lucifer*. The young manager pointed down toward the earth, over which the craft was then skimming, though at no great height.

"It is the lumberyard!" exclaimed Mr. Baxter presently.

"It sure is," assented Tom. "I know I haven't enough stuff to cover as big a blaze as that, but I'll do my best. Fortunately there is no wind to speak of," he added, as he guided the craft in the direction of the fire.

"What has that to do with it—I mean as far as the working of your chemical extinguisher is concerned?" asked Mr. Baxter. "Can't you drop the bomb containers accurately in a wind?"

"Well, the wind has to be allowed for in drop-ping anything from an aeroplane," Tom an-swered. "And, naturally, it does spoil your aim to an extent. But the reason I'm glad there is no wind to speak of is that the chemical blanket I hope to spread over the fire won't be so quickly blown away."

"Oh, I see," said Mr. Baxter. "Well, I'm glad that you will be able to have a successful test of your invention."

"The regular land apparatus is on hand," ob-served Ned, for they were now so near the fire

that they could look down and, in the reflection
from the blaze, could see engines, hose-wagons
and hook and ladder trucks arriving and deploy-
ing to different places of advantage, from which
to fight the lumberyard fire that was now a roar-
ing furnace of flames.

"No skyscraper work needed here," observed
Tom. "But it will give me a chance to use the
latest combination I worked out. I'll try that
first. Are you ready with it, Mr. Baxter?"

"Yes," was the answer.

The young inventor, not heeding the cries of
wonder that arose from below and paying no attention to the uplifted hands and arms pointing
to him, steered his craft to a corner of the yard
where there was a small isolated fire in a pile of
boards. It was Tom's idea to try his new chemical first on this spot to watch the effect. Then
he would turn loose all his other containers of
the chemical mixture that had proved so effective
in other tests.

Attention of those who had gathered to look
at the fire was about evenly divided between the
efforts of the regular department and the pending
action by Tom Swift. The latter was not long in
turning loose his latest sensation.

"Let it go!" he cried to Mr. Baxter, and
down into the seething caldron of flame dropped

a thin sheet-iron container of powerful chemicals.

Leaning over the cockpit of the aircraft, the occupants watched the effect. There was a slight explosion heard, even above the roar of the flames, and the tongues of fire in the section where Tom's extinguisher had fallen died down.

"Good work!" cried Ned.

"No!" answered Tom, shaking his head. "I was a little afraid of this. Not enough carbon dioxide in this mixture. I'll stick to the one I found most effective." For the flames, after momentarily dying down, burst out again in the spot where he had dropped the bomb.

Tom wheeled the airship in a sharp, banking turn, and headed for the heart of the fire in the lumberyard. It was clearly getting beyond the control of the regular department.

"How about you, Ned?" called Tom, for he had given his chum charge of dropping the regular bombs containing a large quantity of the extinguisher Tom had practically adopted.

"All ready," was the answer.

"Let 'em go!" came the command, and down shot the dark, spherical objects. They burst as they hit the ground or the piles of blazing lumber, and at once the powerful gases generated by the mixture of several different chemicals were released.

Again the three in the airship leaned eagerly over the side of the cockpit to watch the effect. It was almost magical in its action.

The bombs had been dropped into the very fiercest heart of the fire, and it was only an instant before their action was made manifest.

"This will do the trick!" cried Ned. "I'm certain it will."

"I didn't have much fear that it wouldn't," said Tom. "But I hoped the other would be better, for it is a much cheaper mixture to make, and that will count when you come to sell it to big cities."

"But the fire is certainly dying down," declared Mr. Baxter.

And this was true. As container after container of the bomb type fell in different parts of the burning lumberyard, while Tom coursed above it, the flames began to be smothered in various sections.

And from the watching crowds, as well as from the hard-working members of the Shopton fire department, came cheers of delight and encouragement as they saw the work of Tom Swift's aerial fire-fighting machine.

For he had, most completely, subdued what threatened to be a great fire, and when the last of his bombs had been dropped, so effective was the blanket of fire-dampening gases spread around that the flames just naturally expired, as it were.

As Tom had said, the absence of wind was in his favor, for the generated gases remained just where they were wanted, directly over the fire like an extinguishing blanket, and were not blown aside as would otherwise have been the case.

And, by the peculiar manner in which his chemicals were mixed, Tom had made them practically harmless for human beings to breathe. Though the fire-killing gases were unpleasant, there was no danger to life in them, and while several of the firemen made wry faces, and one or two were slightly ill from being too close to the chemicals, no one was seriously inconvenienced.

"Well, I guess that's all," said Tom, when the final bomb had been dropped. "That was the last of them, wasn't it, Ned?"

"Yes, but you don't need any more. The fire's out—or what isn't can be easily handled by the hose lines."

"Good!" cried Tom. "But, all the same, I wish I had been able to make the first mixture work."

"Perhaps I can help you with that," suggested Mr. Baxter.

And the following day, after Tom had received

the thanks of the town officials and of the fire department for his work in subduing the lumber-yard blaze, the young inventor called Josephus Baxter in consultation.

"I feel that I need your help," said the young inventor. "You have been at this chemical study longer than I, and I am willing to pay you well for your work. Of course I can't make up to you the loss of your dye formulæ. But while you are waiting for something to turn up in regard to them, you may be glad to assist me."

"I will, and without pay," said the chemist.

But Tom would not hear of that, and together he and Mr. Baxter set about putting the finishing touches to Tom's latest invention.

CHAPTER XIX

"THERE, Tom Swift, it ought to work now!"

Josephus Baxter held up a large laboratory test tube, in which seethed and bubbled some strange mixture, turning from green to purple, then to red, and next to a white, milky mixture.

"Do you think you've hit on the right combination?" asked the young inventor, whose latest idea, the plan of fighting fires in skyscrapers from an airship as a vantage point, was taking up all his spare moments.

"I'm positive of it," said Mr. Baxter. "I've dabbled in chemicals long enough to be certain of this, even if I can't get on the track of the missing dye formulæ."

"That certainly is too bad," declared Tom. "I wish I could help you as much as you have helped me."

"Oh, you have helped me a lot," said the chemist. "You have given me a place to work, much better than the laboratory I had in the old

162

fireworks factory of Field and Melling. And you have paid me, more than liberally, for what little I have done for you."

"You've done a lot for me," declared Tom. "If it had not been for your help this chemical compound would not be nearly as satisfactory as it is, nor as cheap to manufacture, which is a big item."

"Oh, you were on the right track," said Mr. Baxter. "You would have stumbled on it yourself in a short time, I believe. But I will say, Tom Swift, that, between us, we have made a compound that is absolutely fatal to fires. Even a small quantity of it, dropped in the heart of a large blaze, will stop combustion."

"And that's what I want," declared Tom. "I think I shall go ahead now, and proceed with the manufacture of the stuff on a large scale."

"And what do you propose doing with it?" asked Mr. Baxter.

"I'm going to sell the patent and the idea that goes with it to as many large cities as I can," Tom answered. "I'll even manufacture the airships that are needed to carry the stuff over the tops of blazing skyscrapers, dropping it down. I'll supply complete aerial fire-fighting plants."

"And I think you'll do a good business," said the chemist.

It was the conclusion of the final tests of an improved chemical mixture, and the re-action that had taken place in the test tube was the end of the experiment. Success was now again on the side of Tom Swift.

But when that has been said there remains the fact that it was just the other way with the unfortunate Mr. Baxter.

Try as he had, he could not succeed in getting the right chemical combination to perfect the dye process imparted to him by his late French friend. With the disappearance of the secret formulæ went the good luck of Josephus Baxter.

He had worked hard, taking advantage of Tom's generosity, to bring back to his memory the proper manner of mixing certain ingredients, so that permanent dyes of wondrous beauty in coloring would be evolved. But it was all in vain.

"I know who have those formulæ," declared the chemist again and again. "It is those scoundrels, Field and Melling. And they are planning to build up their own dye business with what is mine by right!"

And though Tom, also, believed this, there was no way of proving it.

As the young inventor had said, he was now ready to put his own latest invention on the market. After many tests, aided in some by Mr.

Baxter, a form of liquid fire extinguisher had been made that was superior to any known, and much cheaper to manufacture. Veteran members of fire departments in and about Shopton told Tom so. All that remained was to demonstrate that it would be as effective on a large scale as it was on a small one, and big cities, it was agreed, must, of necessity, add it to their equipment.

"Well, I think I'll give orders to start the works going," said Tom, at the conclusion of the final test. "I have all the ingredients on hand now, and all that remains is to combine them. My airship is all ready, with the bomb-dropping device."

"And I wish you all sorts of luck," said Mr. Baxter. "Now I am going to have another go at my troubles. I have just thought of a possible new way of combining two of the chemicals I need to use. It may be I shall have success."

"I hope so," murmured Tom. He was about to leave the room when Koku, the giant, entered, with a letter in his hand. The big man showed some signs of agitation, and Tom was at once apprehensive about Eradicate.

"Is Rad—has anything happened—shall I get the doctor?"

"Oh, Rad, him all right," answered Koku. "That is him not see *yet,* but mebby soon. Only

I have to chase boy, an' he make faces at me— boy bring this," and the giant held out the envelope.

"Oh!" exclaimed Tom, and he understood now. Messenger boys frequently came to Tom's house or to the shops, and they took delight in poking fun at Koku on account of his size, which made him slow in getting about. The boys delighted to have him chase them, and something like this had evidently just taken place, accounting for Koku's agitation.

"This is for you, Mr. Baxter, not for me," said Tom, as he read the name on the envelope.

"For me!" exclaimed the chemist. "Who could be writing to me? It's a big firm of dye manufacturers," he went on, as he caught a glimpse of the superscription in the upper left hand corner.

Quickly he read the contents of the epistle, and a moment later he gave a joyful cry.

"I'm on the trail! On the trail of those scoundrels at last!" exclaimed Josephus Baxter. "This gives me just the evidence I needed! Now I'll have them where I want them!"

CHAPTER XX

A HEAVY LOAD

Josephus Baxter was so excited by the receipt of the letter which Koku delivered to him that for some seconds Tom Swift could get nothing out of him except the statement:

"I'm on their trail! Now I'm on their trail!"

"What do you mean?" Tom insisted. "Whose trail? What's it all about?"

"It's about Field and Melling! That's who it's about!" exclaimed Mr. Baxter, with a smothered exclamation. "Look, Tom Swift, this letter is addressed to me from one of the biggest dye firms in the world—a firm that is always looking for something new!"

"But if you haven't anything new to give them, of what use is it?" Tom asked, for he knew that the chemist had said his process, stolen, as he claimed, by Field and Melling, was his only new project.

"But I will have something new when I get those secret formulæ away from those scoundrels!" declared Mr. Baxter.

"Yes, but how are you going to do it, when you can't even prove that they have them?" asked Tom.

"Ah, that's the point! Now I think I *can* prove it," declared Mr. Baxter. "Look, Tom Swift! This letter is addressed to me in care of Field and Melling at the office I used to have in their fireworks factory."

"The office from which you were rescued nearly dead," Tom added.

"Exactly. The place where you saved me from a terrible death. Well, if you will notice, this letter was written only two days ago. And it is the first mail I have received as having been forwarded from that address since the fire. I know other mail must have come for me, though."

"What became of it?" asked Tom.

"Those scoundrels confiscated it!" declared the chemist. "But, in some manner, perhaps through the error of a new clerk, this letter was remailed to me here, and now I have it. It is of the utmost importance!"

"In what way?" asked Tom.

"Why, it is directed to me, outside and in, and it makes an inquiry about the very dyes of the lost secret formulæ, one dye in particular."

"I don't quite understand yet," said Tom.

"Well, it's this way," went on Mr. Baxter. "I

had, in the office of Field and Melling, all the papers telling exactly how to make the dyes. After the fire, in which I was rendered unconscious, those papers disappeared.

"The only way in which any one could make the dyes in question was by following the formulæ given in those papers. And now here is a letter, addressed to me from a big firm, asking my prices on a certain dye, which can only be made by the process bequeathed to me by the Frenchman."

"Which means what?" asked Tom.

"It means that Field and Melling must have been writing to this firm on their own hook, offering to sell them some of this dye. But, in some way, my name must have appeared on the letter or papers sent on by the scoundrels, and this big firm replies to *me direct,* instead of to Field and Melling! Even then I would not have benefited if they had confiscated this letter as, I am sure, they have done in the case of others. But, by some slip, I get this.

"And it proves, Tom Swift, that Field and Melling are in possession of my dye formulæ, and that they have tried to dispose of some of the dye to this firm. Not knowing anything of this, the firm replies to me. So now I have direct evidence—just what I wanted—and I can get on the trail of the scoundrels who have cheated me of my rights."

Tom looked at the letter which, it appeared, had been left with Koku by a special delivery boy from the post office. It was an inquiry about certain dyes, and was addressed to Mr. Baxter in care of Field and Melling, the former fireworks firm, which now had started a big dye plant, with offices in the Landmark Building in Newmarket.

"It does look as though you might get at them through this," Tom said, as he handed back the letter. "But I'm afraid you'll have to get further evidence before you could convict them in a court of law—you'll have to show that they actually have possession of your formulæ."

"That's what I wish I could do," said the chemist, somewhat wistfully. His first enthusiasm had been lessened.

"I'll help you all I can," offered Tom. And events were soon to transpire by which the young inventor was to render help to the chemist in a most sensational manner.

"Just now," Tom went on, "I must arrange about getting a large supply of these chemicals made, and then plan for a test in some big city."

"Yes, you have done enough for me," said Mr. Baxter. "But I think now, with this letter as evidence, we'll be able to make a start."

"I agree with you," Tom said. "Why don't you go over to see Mr. Damon? He's a good business man, and perhaps he can advise you. You might also call on that lawyer who does work for Mr. Keith and Mr. Blake. And that reminds me I must call Mary Nestor up and find out when she is coming home. I promised to fetch her in one of the airships."

"I will go and see Mr. Damon," decided Mr. Baxter. "He always gives good advice."

"Even if he does bless everything he sees!" laughed Tom. "But if you're going to see him I'll run you over. I'm going to Waterfield."

"Thanks, I'll be glad to go with you," said the chemist.

Mr. Damon was glad to see his friends, and, when he had listened to the latest developments, he exclaimed with unusual emphasis:

"Bless my law books, Mr. Baxter! but I do believe you're on the right trail at last. Come in, and we'll talk this over."

So Tom left them, traveling on to a distant city where he arranged for a large supply of the chemicals he would need in his extinguisher.

For several days Tom was so busy that he had little time to devote to Mr. Baxter, or even to see him. He learned, however, that the chemist and Mr. Damon were in frequent consultation, and the young inventor hoped something would come of it.

Tom's own plans were going well. He had let several large cities know that he had something new in the way of a fire-fighting machine, and he received several offers to demonstrate it.

He closed with one of these, some distance off, and agreed to fly over in his aircraft and extinguish a fire which was to be started in an old building which had been condemned and was to be destroyed. This was in a city some four hundred miles away and when Ned Newton called on him one afternoon he found Tom busily engaged in loading his sky-craft with a heavy cargo of the newest liquid extinguisher.

"You aren't taking any chances, are you, Tom?" asked Ned.

"What do you mean?"

"I mean you seem to have enough of the liquid 'fire-discourager' to douse any blaze that was ever started."

"No use sending a boy on a man's errand," said Tom. "I'm counting on you to go with me, Ned—you and Mr. Baxter. We leave this afternoon for Denton."

"I'll be with you. Couldn't pass up a chance like that. But here comes Koku, and it looks as if he had something on his mind."

The giant did, indeed, seem to be laboring under the stress of some emotion.

"Oh, Master Tom!" the big man exclaimed when he had got the attention of the young inventor. "Rad—he—he——"

"Has anything happened?" asked Tom, quickly.

"No, not yet. But dat pill man—he say by to-morrow he know if Rad ever will see sunshine more!"

"Oh, the doctor says he'll be able to decide about Rad's eyesight to-morrow, does he?"

"Yes. What so pill man say," repeated Koku.

"Um," mused Tom, "I wish I were going to be here, but I don't see how I can. I must give this test." But it was with a sinking heart as he thought of poor Eradicate that the young inventor proceeded to pile into his airship the largest and heaviest load of chemicals it had ever carried.

CHAPTER XXI

THE LIGHT IN THE SKY

"WELL, what do you say, Tom?" asked Ned, in a low voice.

"She's all right as far as I can see, though she may stagger a bit at the take off."

"It's a pretty heavy load," agreed the young manager, as he and Tom Swift walked about the big fire-fighting airship *Lucifer,* which had been rolled outside the hangar. "But still I think she'll take it, especially since you've tuned up the motor so it's at least twenty per cent. more powerful than it was."

"Perhaps you'd better leave me out," suggested Mr. Baxter, who had been helping the boys. "I'm not a feather weight, you know."

"I need you with us," said Tom. "I want your expert opinion on the effect the new chemicals have on the flames."

"Well, I'd like to come," admitted the chemist, "for it will be a valuable experience for me. But I don't want an accident up in the air."

174

"Trust Tom Swift for that!" cried Ned. "If he says his aircraft will do the trick, it positively will."

"How about leaving me out?" asked Mr. Damon. "I'm not an expert in anything, as far as I know."

"You are in keeping us cheerful. And we may need you to bless things if there's a slip-up anywhere," laughed Tom, for Mr. Damon had been invited to be one of the party.

"I don't so much mind a slip-up," said Mr. Damon, "as I do a slip down. That's where it hurts! However, I'll take a chance with you, Tom Swift. It won't be the first one—and I guess it won't be the last."

The work of getting the big airship ready for what was to be a conclusive test of her fire-fighting abilities from the clouds proceeded rapidly. As has been related, Tom had perfected, with the help of Mr. Baxter, a combination of chemicals which was effective in putting out a fire when dropped into the blaze from above. Quantities of this combination had been stored in metal containers which Tom had at first styled "bombs," but which he now called "aerial grenades."

The manner of dropping the grenades was, on the whole, similar to the manner in which bombs were dropped from airships during the Great

War, but Tom had made several improvements in this plan.

These improvements had to do with the releasing of the bombs, or, in this case, grenades. It is not easy to drop or throw something from a swiftly moving airship so that it will hit an object on the ground. During the war aviators had to train for some time before becoming even approximately accurate.

Tom Swift decided that to leave this matter to chance or to the eye of the occupant of an airship was too indefinite. Accordingly he invented a machine, something like a range-finder for big guns. With this it was a comparatively easy matter to drop a grenade at almost any designated place.

To accomplish this it was necessary to take into consideration the speed of the airship, its height above the ground, the velocity of the wind, the weight of the grenades, and other things of this sort. But by an intricate mathematical process Tom solved the problem, so that it was only necessary to set certain pointers and levers along a slide rule in the cockpit of the craft. Then when the releasing catch was pressed, the grenades would drop down just about where they were most needed.

"I think everything is ready," said Tom, when he had taken a last look over his craft, making sure that all the chemical grenades were in place. "If you will be ready, gentlemen, we will take our places and start in about half an hour," he added. "I want to say good-bye to my father, and cheer up Rad—if I can."

"The doctor will know to-morrow, will he?" asked Mr. Damon.

"Yes. And I'm sorry I will not be here to listen to the report," said Tom. "Though I am almost afraid to receive it," he added in a low voice. "I shall blame myself if Rad is to go through the remainder of his life blind."

"It couldn't be helped," said Ned. "We'll hope for the best."

"Yes," agreed Tom, "that's all we can do— hope for the best. By the way," he went on, turning to Mr. Baxter, "are you any nearer fastening the guilt on those two rascals, Field and Melling?"

"Bless my prosecuting attorney, no!" exclaimed Mr. Damon. "Those are the slickest scoundrels I ever tackled! They're like a flea. Once you think you have them where you want them, and they're on the other side of the table, skipping around."

"I've about given up," said Mr. Baxter, in discouraged tones. "I guess my dye formulæ are gone forever."

"Don't say that!" exclaimed Tom. "Once I get this fire matter off my hands, I'm going to tackle the problem myself. We'll either make those fellows sorry they ever meddled in this matter, or we'll get up a new combination of dyes that will put them out of business!"

"Bless my Easter eggs, I'm glad to hear you talk that way!" cried Mr. Damon.

"Well, Rad, I'll expect to see you up and around when I get back," said Tom to his old servant, as he stepped into the sick room to say good-bye.

"Oh, is yo' goin', Massa Tom?" asked the colored man, turning his bandaged head in the direction of the beloved voice.

"Yes. I'm going to try out a new scheme of mine—the fire extinguisher, you know."

"De same one whut fizzed up, an'—an' busted me in de eyes, Massa Tom?"

"Yes, Rad, I'm sorry to say, it's the same one."

"Oh, shucks now, Massa Tom! whut's use worryin'?" laughed Rad. "I suah will be all right when yo' gits back. De doctor man—de 'pill man' dat giant calls him—says I'll suah be better."

"Of course you will," declared Tom, but his heart sank when he saw Mrs. Baggert remove the bandages and he caught sight of Rad's burned face and the eyes that had to be kept closed if ever they were again to look on the sunshine and flowers. "And when I come back, Rad, I'll stage a little fire for your benefit, and show you how quickly I can put it out."

"Ha! dat's whut I wants to see, Massa Tom, I suah does like to see fires!" chuckled Eradicate. "Mah ole mule, Boomerang—does yo' 'member him, Massa Tom?"

"Of course, Rad!"

"Well, Boomerang he liked fires, too. Liked 'em so much I jest couldn't git him past 'em lots ob times! But run 'long, Massa Tom. Yo' ain't got no time to waste on an ole culled man whut's seen his best days. Yas-sir, I reckon I'se seen mah best days," and the smile died from the honest, black face.

"Oh, don't talk like that!" cried Tom, as cheerfully as he could. "You've got a lot of work in you yet, Rad. Hasn't he, Koku?" and the young inventor appealed to the giant, who seldom left the side of his former enemy.

"Rad good man—him an' me do lots work—next week mebby," said Koku, smiling very broadly.

"That's the way to talk!" exclaimed Tom, and he laughed a little though his heart was far from light.

And then, having seen to the final details, he took his place in the big airship with Ned, Mr. Damon and Josephus Baxter. The craft carried the largest possible load of fire extinguishing chemicals.

As Tom had feared, the *Lucifer* staggered a bit in "taking off" late that afternoon when the start was made for the distant city of Denton, where the first real test was to be made under the supervision and criticism of the fire department. But once the craft was aloft she rode on a level keel.

"I guess we're all right," Tom said. But to make certain he circled several times over his own landing field, that a good place to come down might be assured if something unforeseen developed.

However, all went well, and then the course was straightened for the distant city.

"We'll go right over Newmarket, sha'n't we, Tom?" asked Ned, as the speed of the *Lucifer* increased.

"Yes. And I wish I had time to stop and see Mary, but I haven't. It's getting dark fast, and we ought to arrive at our destination early in the morning. The test has been set by the committee for ten o'clock."

They settled themselves comfortably in the big craft for a long night trip, and Mr. Damon was just going to bless something or other when he pointed off into the distance.

"Look, Tom!" cried the eccentric man. "See that light in the sky!"

"Seems to be a fire," observed Ned.

"It *is* a fire!" shouted Mr. Baxter. "And it's in Newmarket, if I'm any judge."

Tom Swift did not answer, but he shoved forward the gasolene lever of his controls, and the *Lucifer* shot ahead through the air while the red, angry glow deepened in the evening sky.

CHAPTER XXII

TRAPPED

WHILE Tom Swift was loading the *Lucifer* for
her trip and the fire extinguishing test to occur
the next morning, quite a different scene was taking place in the home of Jasper Blake, the uncle
of Mary Nestor, where she had gone to spend a
few weeks.

"Well, are you all ready, Mary?" asked her
aunt, and it was about the same time that Ned
Newton asked that same question of Tom Swift.
Only Tom was in Shopton, and Mary was in
Newmarket, and Tom was setting off on an air
voyage, while Mary was only preparing to take
a car downtown to do some shopping.

"Yes, Aunt, I'm all ready," Mary answered.
"But I may be a bit late getting home."

"Why?" asked Mrs. Blake.

"I promised Uncle Barton I'd stop and call on
him at his office," Mary replied. "He has something he wants me to take home to mother when
I go to-morrow."

"I shall be sorry to see you go back," said Mrs.

Blake. "But I imagine there will be those in Shopton who will be glad to see you return, Mary."

"Yes, mother wrote that she and dad were getting a bit lonesome," the girl casually replied, as she adjusted her veil.

"Yes, and some one else. Ah, Mary, you are a very lucky girl!" laughed her aunt, while Mary turned aside so she would not see her own blushes in the mirror.

"I thought Tom was going to call and take you home in his airship, Mary," went on her relative.

"So he is, I believe, on his way back from a city where he is going to be to-morrow making a big fire test. I am to wait for him until to-morrow afternoon. But now I really must go shopping, or all the bargains will be taken. Is there any word you want to send to Uncle Barton?"

"No," answered Mrs. Blake. "Though you might tell him to stop poking fun at your Uncle Jasper for having invested money in the Land-mark Building. It's getting on your Uncle Jasper's nerves," she added.

"Uncle Barton never can give up a joke, once he thinks he has one," said Mary. "But I'll tell him to stop pestering Uncle Jasper."

"Please do," urged Mary's aunt, and then the girl left.

Mary's uncle, Barton Keith, with whom Tom Swift had been associated during the undersea search, had offices in the Landmark Building, but his home was in an adjoining suburb.

The girl was pleased with the results of her shopping, and at the close of the afternoon she stopped at the Landmark Building and was soon being shot up in the elevator to the floor where Barton Keith had his offices.

Though Mr. Keith had refrained from investing in the Landmark Building and though he laughed at Mary's Uncle Jasper for having done so, this did not prevent him from having a suite of offices in the big structure which, as we already know, was owned in large part by Field and Melling.

"Ah, Mary! Come in!" exclaimed Mr. Keith, welcoming Tom Swift's sweetheart. "It is so late I was afraid you weren't coming, and I was about to close the office and go home."

"You must blame the bargain sales for my delay," laughed Mary. "I hope I haven't kept you waiting."

"No, I still had a few things to do. One was to write a letter to your Uncle Jasper, telling him

I had heard of another fire trap that was open to investors."

"Oh, and that reminds me I must tell you not to push Uncle Jasper too far!" warned Mary.

"Ha! Ha!" laughed Uncle Barton. "He made fun of me for going on the undersea search with Tom Swift. But I made good on that, and that's more than he can say about his Landmark Building deal!"

"But don't exasperate him too much!" begged Mary. "By the way, what are they doing to this building? I see the stairways and some of the elevator shafts all littered with building material."

"They are trying to make it fireproof," answered her uncle. "It's rather late to try that now, but they've got either to do it or stand a big increase in insurance rates. I'm glad I'm out of it. But now, Mary, take an easy chair until I finish some work, and then I'll walk out with you."

Mary took a seat near one of the front windows, whence she could look down into the now fast-darkening streets. She could see the supper crowds hurrying home, and out in the corridor of the big skyscraper could be heard the banging of elevator doors as the office tenants, one after another, left for the day.

Suddenly there was more commotion than usual, followed by the sound of broken glass. Then came a cry of:

"Fire! Fire!"

Mary sprang to her feet with a gasp of alarm, and her uncle rushed past her to the door leading into the hall outside his offices. As he opened the door a cloud of smoke rushed toward him and Mary, causing them to choke and gasp.

Mr. Keith closed the door a moment, and when he opened it again the smoke in the hall seemed less dense.

"It probably is only a slight blaze among some of the material the workmen are using," he said. "Come, Mary, we'll get out."

Pausing only to swing shut the door of his heavy safe and to stuff some valuable papers into his pocket, Mr. Keith advanced and, taking Mary by the arm, led her into the hall. The smoke was increasing again, and distant shouts and cries could be heard, mingled with the breaking of glass.

Mr. Keith rang the elevator buzzer several times, but when no car came up the shaft in response to his summons he turned to his niece and said:

"We'll try the stairs. It's only ten stories

down, and going down isn't anything like coming up."

"Oh, indeed I can walk!" said Mary. "Let's hurry out!"

They turned toward the stairway, which wound around the elevator shafts, but such a cloud of hot, stifling smoke rolled up that it sent them back, choking and gasping for breath.

And then, as they stood there, up the elevator shafts, which were veritable chimneys, came more hot smoke, mingled with sparks of fire.

"Trapped!" gasped Mr. Keith, and he pulled Mary back toward his offices to get away from the choking, stifling smoke. "We're trapped!"

CHAPTER XXIII

TO THE RESCUE

"Uncle! Uncle Barton!" faltered Mary, as she clung to Mr. Keith. "Can't we get down the stairs?"

"I'm afraid not, Mary," he answered, and he closed the door of his office to keep out the smoke that was ever increasing.

"And won't the elevators come for us?"

"They don't seem able to get up," was his reply. "Probably the fire started in the bottom of the shafts, and they act just like flues, drawing up the flames and smoke."

"Then we must try the fire escapes!" exclaimed Mary, and she started toward the front window, pulling her uncle across the room after her.

"Mary, there aren't—aren't any fire escapes!" he said hoarsely.

"No fire escapes!" The girl turned paler than before.

"No, not an escape as far as I know. You see, this was thought to be a fireproof building at first and small attention was given to escapes. Then the law stepped in and the owners were ordered to put up regular escapes. They have started the work, but just now the old escapes have been torn down and the new ones are not yet in place."

"Oh, but Uncle Barton! can't we do *something?*" cried Mary. "There must be some way out! Let's try the elevators again, or the stairs!"

Before Mr. Keith could stop her Mary had opened the door into the hall. To the agreeable surprise of her uncle there seemed to be less smoke now.

"We may have a chance!" he cried, and he rushed out. "Hurry!"

Frantically he pushed the button that summoned the elevators. Down below, in the elevator shafts, could be heard the roar and crackle of flames.

"Let's try the stairs!" suggested Mary. "They seem to be free now."

She started down the staircase which went in square turns about the battery of elevators, and her uncle followed. But they had not more than reached the first landing when a roll of black, choking smoke, mingled with sparks of fire, surged into their faces.

"Back, Mary! Back!" cried Mr. Keith, and he dragged the impetuous girl with him to their own corridor, and back into his offices which, for the time being, were comparatively free from the choking vapor.

"We must try the windows, Uncle Barton! We must!" cried Mary. "Surely there is some way down—maybe by dropping from ledge to ledge!"

Her uncle shook his head. Then he opened the window and looked out. As he did so there arose from the streets below the cries of many voices, mingled with the various sounds of fire apparatus —the whistles of engines, the clang of gongs, and the puffing of steamers.

"The firemen are here! They'll save us!" cried Mary, as she heard the noises in the street below. "We can leap into the life nets."

"There isn't a life net made, nor men who could retain it, to hold up a person jumping from the tenth story," said her uncle. "Our only chance is to wait for them to subdue the fire."

"Isn't there a back way down, Uncle Barton?"

"No, Mary!" He closed the window for, open as it was, the draft created served to suck smoke into the office, and Mary was coughing.

Uncle and niece faced each other. Trapped indeed they were, unless the fire, which was now raging all through the building, with the stairs and elevator shafts as a center, could be subdued.

That the city fire department was doing its best was not to be doubted.

"We can only wait—and hope," said Mr. Keith solemnly.

Mary gave a gasp. Her uncle thought she was going to burst into tears, but she bravely conquered herself and faced him with what was meant to be a smile. But it is difficult to smile with quivering lips, and Mary soon gave up the attempt.

Mr. Keith went over to the water cooler—one of those inverted large glass bottles—and looked to see how much water it contained.

"It's nearly full," he said.

"What good will it do?" asked Mary. "This fire is beyond a little water like that."

"Yes, but it will serve to keep our handkerchiefs wet so we can breathe through them if the smoke gets too thick," was his reply.

"It begins to look as if we'd need to try that soon," said Mary, and she pointed to thick smoke curling in under the door.

"Yes," agreed her uncle. "It's getting worse."

Hardly had he spoken when there came a rush of feet in the corridor outside his office door. Then a voice exclaimed:

"We're trapped! We can't get down either the stairs or the elevators!"

"It can't be possible!" said another voice. "Something must be done! Help! Help! Take us out of here!"

"Foolish cowards!" murmured Mr. Keith, and then the door of his office was violently opened and two men rushed in. They were strangers to Mary and her uncle.

"Isn't there any way out of this fire trap?" cried one of the men. "Are there any fire escapes at your windows?"

"None," said Mr. Keith.

"This is all your fault, Melling!" cried the smaller of the two men, whose voice, in loudness and depth of pitch, was out of all proportion to his size. "All your fault! I told you we should have those new fire escapes!"

"And you were the one, Field, who objected to the cost of fire escapes when you found what the charge would be," retorted the other. "You said we didn't need to waste that money, if the building was fire-proof."

"But it isn't, Melling! It isn't!" yelled the other.

"We're finding that out too late!" came the retort. "But I'm not going to die here like a rat in a trap!" And he raised the window and leaned out and yelled, "Help! Help! Help!"

"Don't do that," said Mr. Keith, coming over to

close the casement. "They can't hear you down below, and opening the window will only fill this place with smoke. Are you Field and Melling?"

"Yes, of the Consolidated Dye Company," was the answer from the big man. "We are also part owners of this building, but I wish we weren't."

"It is a pretty poor specimen of a modern building," said Mr. Keith. "You have offices here, haven't you?" he went on. "I remember to have seen your names on the directory."

"We're on the floor above," was the answer from Field. "We were in a rear room, going over some accounts, and we didn't know anything was wrong until we smelled smoke. We tried to get down, and managed to come, by way of the stairs, as far as this floor," he explained quickly.

"You can't go any farther," said Mr. Keith. "All there is to do is to wait for the firemen."

"Suppose they never come?" whined Melling.

"Oh, they'll come!" asserted Mary's uncle, but he spoke more to quiet her alarm than because he really believed it, for the Landmark Building was a seething furnace of flame centering in and about the elevator shafts and stairs.

Meanwhile Tom and his companions in the airship had seen the red glow in the evening sky, and in another minute the young inventor had turned his craft more directly toward it.

"It surely is in Newmarket," said Mr. Damon. "Right in the center of the city, too. There's one big building there—the Landmark."

"Looks as if that was afire," said Ned quickly. "Hasn't some relative of Mary's an office there, Tom?"

"Yes. Mr. Keith. And her other uncle, Jasper Blake, is also interested in the building. It's the Landmark all right!" cried Tom, as his craft rose higher and advanced nearer the blaze.

"What are you going to do?" yelled Mr. Damon, as he saw the young inventor head directly toward a spouting mushroom of flame, which showed that the fire had broken through the roof. "What are you going to do?"

"Go to the rescue!" answered Tom Swift. "I couldn't ask a better opportunity to try my new extinguisher! Sit tight, every one!"

CHAPTER XXIV

A STRANGE DISCOVERY

ONCE it became evident to the occupants of the airship what Tom Swift's plans were, they all prepared to help him. Previous to the trip certain duties had been assigned to each one, duties which were to be exercised when Tom gave the exhibition of his new aerial fire-fighting apparatus at the set fire before the fire department of Denton.

This preparation now stood the young inventor in good stead, for there was no confusion aboard the *Lucifer* when she winged her way toward the burning Landmark Building, where the flames were continually spouting higher and higher as they rushed through the roof, directly above the stairway well and elevator shafts.

So far the flames had confined themselves to this central part of the big structure, but it was only a question of time when they would spread out on all sides, licking up the remainder of the pile. And, for the most part, the firemen on the ground were at a great disadvantage.

They had run in lines as near as they could get to the center of the blaze, and had also attached hose to the standpipes inside the building. But this last effort was wasted, as developed later, for there was no one in the building to direct the nozzle ends of the hose attached to the standpipes on the different floors. Also the fierce heat fairly melted the pipes themselves in the vicinity of the elevator shafts, and there was no automatic sprinkling system in the building.

This was the situation, then, when Tom in his airship loaded with fire-extinguishing chemicals, headed for the blaze. And this, also, was the desperate situation that confronted Mary Nestor and her uncle, Barton Keith, as well as Amos Field and Jason Melling. Those unscrupulous and cowardly men were in a veritable panic of fear, which contrasted strangely with the calm, resigned attitude of Mary and her uncle.

"We must get out! Some one must save us!" yelled Field.

"Jump from the window!" cried Melling.

"No, I can't permit that!" declared Mr. Keith, standing in their path. "It would be sure death! As it is, there may be a chance."

"A chance? How?" asked Field. "Listen to that!"

Through the closed door of Mr. Keith's office

could be heard the roar and crackle of flames, while the very air was now stifling and hot, filled with acrid smoke.

"We can only wait," said Mr. Keith, and he wet Mary's handkerchief in the water and handed it to her to bind over her face.

"Is everything all right, Ned?" called Tom, as he turned on a little more power, so that the *Lucifer* lunged ahead toward the great pillar of fire that now reddened the sky for miles around.

"All ready," was the answer. "You only have to give the word when you want us to let go."

"Let go!" cried Mr. Damon. "Bless my umbrella, Tom! We don't have to jump out, do we?"

"He means to let go the extinguisher grenades," said Mr. Baxter. "Shall we let them all go at once, Tom?" asked the chemist.

"No, drop half when I shoot over the first time. We'll see what effect they have, and then come back with the rest."

"That's the idea!" cried Ned. "Well, give us the word when you're ready, Tom."

"I will," was the answer of the young inventor, and with keen eyes he began to set the automatic gages so those in charge of the grenades would be able to drop them most effectively.

The flames were mounting higher and higher

above the ill-fated Landmark Building. It was a "land-mark" now, for miles around—a fearsome mark, indeed.

"I hope every one is out of the place," said Ned, as the airship approached nearer and the fierceness of the fire was more manifest.

"Bless my thermometer, you're right!" exclaimed Mr. Damon. "I don't see how any one could live in that furnace."

Seen from above it appeared that the fire was engulfing the whole building, while, as a matter of fact, only the central portion was yet blazing. But it was only a question of time when the remainder would ignite.

And it was to this fact—that the fire was rushing up the stairway and elevator shafts as up a chimney—that Mary and her uncle, as well as Field and Melling, owed their temporary safety.

Had Tom known that the girl he loved was in such direful danger, it is doubtful if his hand would have been as steady as it was on throttle and steering wheel. But not a muscle or nerve quivered. To Tom it was but carrying out a prearranged task. He was going to extinguish a great blaze, or attempt to do so, by means of his aerial fire-fighting apparatus. And his previous tests had given him confidence in his device. His one regret was that the fire department of the city that was contemplating the purchase of certain rights in his invention could not witness what he was about to do.

"But they'll hear of it," declared Ned, when Tom voiced this idea to his chum.

Nearer and nearer to the up-spouting column of flames the airship winged her way. Tense and alert, Tom sat at the wheel guiding his craft with her load of fire-defying chemicals. Behind him were Ned, Mr. Damon and Mr. Baxter, ready to drop the grenades at the word.

"Getting close, Tom!" called Ned, as they could all feel the heat of the conflagration in the Landmark Building, which now seemed doomed. "You'll not dare cross it too low down, will you?"

"No, I'll have to keep pretty well up," was the answer. "There's a current of air over that fire which might turn us turtle."

Heat creates a draft, sucking in colder air from below, and making an upward-rushing column which, in the case of a big blaze, is very powerful. Tom knew he had to avoid this.

It was now almost time to act. In another few seconds they would be sailing directly into the path of the up-spouting flames. Realizing that to do this at too low an elevation would result in disaster, Tom sent his craft upward at a sharp angle. Then he turned to call to his companions.

"Be ready when I give the word!"

"All set and ready!" answered Ned, and the others signified their attention to the command that soon was to be given.

Having attained what he considered a sufficient elevation, Tom headed the *Lucifer* straight toward the up-spouting column of fire and smoke. If ever his craft of the air was to justify her name it was now!

Straight and true as an arrow she headed for the fiery pillar! Hotter and hotter grew the air! The darkness of the night was lighted by the awful fire, which rendered objects in the street clear and distinct. But Tom and his friends had little time for such observation.

"Get ready!" cried the young inventor, as he felt a rush of heat across his face, partly protected, as it was, by great goggles.

"All ready!" shouted Ned.

"Let go!" cried Tom, and with a click of springs the fire extinguishers dropped from the bottom of the *Lucifer* into the very heart of the flames in the Landmark Building.

There was a blast as from a furnace seventy times heated, a choking and gasping for breath on the part of the occupants of the airship, a shriveling, as it seemed, of the naked flesh, and then, when it appeared that all of them must be engulfed in the great heat, the airship passed out of the zone of fire.

A rush of cool air followed, reviving them all, and then, when out of the swirls of smoke, Ned, looking back, cried:

"Good work, Tom! Good work!"

"Did we hit it?" cried the young inventor.

"She's half gone!" declared Mr. Baxter. "Can you give her the rest of the load?"

"I'm going to try!" declared Tom.

"Bless my bank balance!" shouted Mr. Damon, "are we going through that awful furnace again?"

"It will not be so bad this time," observed Ned. "The fire is half out now. Tom's stuff did the trick!"

Indeed it was evident, as Tom sent the *Lucifer* around in a sharp turn, that the fire had been largely smothered by the gas that now lay over it like a wet blanket. But there was still some fire spouting up.

"Give her all we have!" yelled Tom, as, once more, he prepared to cross the zone of fire.

"Right," sang out Ned.

Once more the *Lucifer* swept over the burning building. Down shot the remaining grenades, falling into the mass of flames and bursting, though the reports could not be heard because

of the tumult in the streets below. For the firemen and spectators had seen the sudden dying
down of the fire, they had caught sight of a
shadowy shape in the night, hovering over the
blazing building, and they wondered what it all
meant.

"How is it?" asked Tom, as he guided the
craft back to get a view of his work.

"That settles it!" answered Ned. "There isn't
fire enough now to broil a beefsteak!"

This was not exactly true, for the blaze was not
entirely subdued. But the flames had all been
killed off in the higher parts of the Landmark
Building, and what remained could easily be dealt
with by the firemen on the ground. They proceeded to make short work of the remainder of
the conflagration, the while wondering who had
so effectively aided them from the clouds.

"Well," observed Tom, as he saw how effectively he had smothered the great fire, "it's of
no use to go on now. I haven't an ounce of
chemical left on board. I can't give the demonstration that I planned for to-morrow."

"You've given a better demonstration here than
you ever could have in the other city," declared
Mr. Baxter. "I fancy this will be all the test
needed, Tom Swift!"

"Perhaps. I hope so. But we may as well

land and see from the ground the effect of our work. I'd also like to inquire if any one was hurt. Let's go down."

It was rather ticklish work, making a landing in the midst of a populous city, and at night. But as it happened, there had been a number of buildings razed in the vicinity of the Landmark structure, and there was a large, vacant level space. Also several of the city's fire department searchlights were focused around the burning structure, and when it became evident that an airship was going to land—though as yet none guessed whose it was—the searchlights were turned on the vacant spot and Tom was able to make a good landing, his own powerful searchlight giving effective aid.

"What did you do that put out the fire?" demanded the chief of the Newmarket department, as he rushed up with a crowd of others when Tom and his friends alighted.

"I dropped a few grenades down that chimney," modestly answered the young inventor.

"A few grenades! Say, you must have turned a whole river of them loose!" cried the delighted chief. "It doused the fire quicker than I ever saw one put out in all my life!"

"I'm glad I was successful," said Tom. "But was any one in the building?"

"Yes, a few," answered a policeman, who was trying to keep the crowd back from the airship. "They're bringing them out now."

"Killed?" gasped Tom.

"No. But some of them are badly hurt," the officer answered. "There was one young lady and a man named Barton Keith——"

"Barton Keith!" shouted Tom, springing forward. "Was he—— Who was the young lady? I—I——"

But at that moment there was a stir in the crowd about the building, in which only a little fire now remained, and through the throng came a disheveled and smoke-blackened young lady and a man whose clothing was also greatly disarrayed.

"Mary!" cried the young inventor.

"Tom!" gasped Mary Nestor. "How did you get here?"

"I came to put out the fire," was the answer, and Tom cooled down now that he saw Mary was unharmed. "How did you happen to be in the building?"

"I was in Uncle Barton's office when the fire broke out," answered Mary, "and we were trapped. We had to stay there, with two men from the floor above."

"Yes, and if they had stayed with us they wouldn't have been hurt," said Mr. Keith. "But, as it was, they rushed out and tried to get down the stairs. They were caught in the draft and badly burned, I believe. They are bringing them out now."

Two stretchers, on which lay inert forms, were borne through the now silent crowd by firemen and police officers, and taken to waiting ambulances.

"That's Field and Melling," said Mr. Keith to Tom. "They had offices just above me, and they were trapped, as were Mary and I. They acted like big cowards, too, though I hope they're not badly hurt. We stayed inside my office, and we were just giving up the hope of rescue when the fire seemed suddenly to die down."

"I should say it was sudden!" cried the enthusiastic local chief. "It was the chemicals from this young man's airship that did the trick!"

"Oh, Tom, was it your new machine?" asked Mary.

"Yes," was the answer. "I was on my way to give a test to-morrow in Denton when I saw this fire. I didn't know you were in it, though, Mary."

"Oh, but I'm glad you came," she said. "It was just—awful!" and she clung to Tom's arm, trembling.

When Field and Melling, whose rash conduct

had caused them to be severely but not fatally burned, had been taken to a hospital and the fire was declared to be practically out, Tom made arrangements to leave his airship in the city field all night.

"And you and your friends can come to Uncle Jasper's house," said Mary.

"Of course!" said Uncle Jasper himself, who had arrived on the scene, attracted to the fire by the news that his niece and Mr. Keith were in danger. "Lots of room! Come along! We'll celebrate your rescue!"

So the crew of the fire-fighting *Lucifer* went with Mary, while the firemen, after again thanking Tom most enthusiastically, kept on playing, as a precaution, their streams of water on the still hot building.

Only the central portion of the structure, the stairs and elevator shafts, were burned away. The strong upward draft had kept the fire from spreading much to either side.

"It certainly was a fierce blaze, and I'm glad my chemicals took such prompt effect," said Tom. "I shall not fear any test after this."

It was the day following the night of excitement, and Tom and his friends, at the invitation of the fire department of Newmarket, were inspecting what was left of the Landmark Building

—and there was considerable left—though access to the upper floors was to be had only by ladders, down which Mary and her uncle, Barton Keith, had been carried.

"Here are my offices," said Mr. Keith, who accompanied Tom, Ned, Mr. Damon and Mr. Baxter, as he ushered them into his suite of rooms.

"Bless my fountain pen! nothing is burned here," cried the eccentric man.

"No, the flames just shot upward," explained the fire chief, who was leading the party. "But I think those chemicals of yours would have been just as effective, Mr. Swift, if the fire had mushroomed out more."

"It was hot enough as it was," answered Tom, with a grim laugh.

"Bless my thermometer, too hot—too hot by far!" exclaimed Tom Swift's eccentric friend, and to this Ned nodded an amused agreement.

An exclamation from Mr. Baxter attracted the attention of all in Mr. Keith's office. The chemist picked up from the floor a bundle of papers.

"Here is a bundle of documents that some one has dropped, Mr. Keith," he said. "I guess you forgot to put it in your safe. Why—why—no—they aren't yours! They're *mine!* Here are my missing dye formulæ! The secret papers I've been searching for so long! The ones I thought Field and Melling had!" cried Mr. Baxter. "How—how did they get here?" and, wonderingly, he looked at the bundle of papers he had discovered in such a strange manner.

CHAPTER XXV

THE LIGHT OF DAY

"WHAT'S that? Your dye formulæ here in my office?" cried Mr. Keith, for he had heard something of the chemist's loss, though he did not directly associate Field and Melling with it.

"That's what this is! The very papers, containing all the rare secrets, for which I have been so at a loss!" cried the delighted old man. "Now I can give to the world the dyes for which it has long been waiting! Oh, Tom Swift, you did more than you knew when you put out this fire!" and he hugged the bundle of smoke-smelling papers to his breast.

"But how did they get here?" asked the young inventor. "I know that Field and Melling had offices in this building. They were starting a new dye concern, and, though Mr. Baxter and I suspected them of having stolen his secret, we couldn't prove it."

"But we can now!" cried Mr. Baxter. "Though I don't know that I'll bother even to accuse them, as long as I have back my precious papers. I see how it happened. They had the formulæ in their office. They rushed out with the documents, and, when they found they couldn't get past this floor, they went into Mr. Keith's office. There, in their excitement, they dropped the papers, and you put the fire out just in time, Tom, or they'd have been burned beyond hope of saving. You have given me back something almost as valuable as life, Tom Swift!"

"I'm glad I could render you that service," said the young inventor. "And I had no idea, when I dropped the chemicals, that I was saving someone even more valuable than your secret formulæ," and they all knew he referred to Mary Nestor.

An examination of the papers found on Mr. Keith's office floor showed that not one of the dye secrets was missing. Thus Mr. Baxter came into possession of his own again, and when Field and Melling were sufficiently recovered they were charged with the theft of the papers. The charge was proved, and, in addition, other accusations were brought against them which insured their remainder in jail for a considerable period.

As Mr. Baxter had suspected, Field and Melling had, indeed, robbed him of his dye formulæ papers. They learned that he possessed them, and they invited him to a night conference with the purpose of robbing him. The fire in their factory was an accident, of which they took advantage to make it appear that the chemist lost his papers in the blaze. But they had taken them, and though they did not mean to leave poor Baxter to his fate, that would have been the result of their selfish action had not Tom and Ned come to the rescue. And it was of this "putting over" that Field and Melling had boasted, the time Tom overheard their talk at Meadow Inn.

As Mr. Baxter guessed, the letter delivered to him at Tom's place was one that the two scoundrels would have retained, as they had others like it, if they had seen it. But a new clerk forwarded it, and the evidence it contained helped to convict Field and Melling.

As for the Landmark Building, while badly damaged, it would have been worse burned but for Tom's prompt action. And though he was more than glad that he had been on hand, he rather regretted that he could not give the test for which he had set out.

Eventually the building was made more nearly fire-proof and the fire-escapes were rebuilt, and Mr. Blake did not lose his money, as he had feared, though Barton Keith said it was more owing to Tom Swift's good luck than to Mr. Blake's management.

But, as it developed, nothing could have been more opportune than Tom's action, for word of his quenching a bigger blaze than he would have had to encounter in the official test reached the Denton fire department. As a result there was a conference, and, after only a nominal showing of his apparatus, it was adopted by a unanimous vote.

But this occurred some time afterward, for, following his rescue of Mary Nestor and her uncle and the saving of the lives of Field and Melling, as well as others in the building, by his prompt smothering of the fire, Tom returned to Shopton.

He and his companions went in the *Lucifer,* minus, now, the big load of chemicals, and on landing near the hangar Tom was surprised to see Koku the giant running toward him. The big man showed every symptom of great excitement as he cried:

"Oh, Master Tom! He see the light ob day! He see the light ob day now! Oh, so glad! So glad!"

"Who sees the light of day?" asked the young inventor.

"Black Rad! Eradicate! Him eyes all better now! Pill man take off cloth. Rad—he see light ob day!"

"Oh, I'm so glad! So thankful!" cried Tom. "How I've wished for this! Is it really true, Koku?"

"Sure true! Pill man say Rad see K O now."

The giant, doubtless, meant "O K," but Tom understood. And it was true, as he learned more directly a little later.

When Tom entered the room where Rad had been kept in the dark ever since the explosion, the colored man looked at his master with seeing eyes, though the apartment was still but dimly lighted.

"I's all right ag'in now, Massa Tom!" cried Rad. "See fine! I's all ready to make more smellin' stuff to put out fires!"

"You won't have to, Rad!" cried Tom joyfully. "My chemical extinguisher is completed, and you did your share in making it a success. But I never would have felt like claiming credit for it if you had been—had been left in the dark."

"No mo' dark, Massa Tom!" said Eradicate. "I kin see now as good as eber, an' yo'-all won't hab to 'pend on dat lazy good-fo'-nuffin cocoa-nut!" and he chuckled as he looked at the giant.

"Huh! Lazy!" retorted the big man. "I show you—black coon!"

"By golly!" laughed Rad. "Him an' me good friends now, Massa Tom. Neber I fuss wif

Koku any mo'!   He suah was good to me when I
had to stay in de dark!"

Of course it would be too much to hope that
Koku and Eradicate never again quarreled, but
for a long time their warm friendship was a thing
at which to marvel, considering the past.

"Well, I guess this settles it," said Tom to Ned
one day, after going over the day's mail.

"Settles what, Tom?"

"My aerial fire-fighting apparatus. Here's
word from the National Fire Underwriters Association that they have adopted it, and there will
be a big reduction of rates in all cities where it is
a part of the fire department equipment.   It's
been as great a success as Mr. Baxter's new dye."

"Yes, and he has had wonderful success with
that.   But what are you going to do now, Tom?
What new line of endeavor are you going to aim
at?"

Tom arose and reached for his hat.

"I am now going," he said, with a grin, "to see
somebody on private business."

"You are going to see Mary Nestor!" broke
out Ned.

"I am," said Tom.

And he did.

THE END

This Isn't All!

Would you like to know what became of the good friends you have made in this book?

Would you like to read other stories continuing their adventures and experiences, or other books quite as entertaining by the same author?

On the *reverse side* of the wrapper which comes with this book, you will find a wonderful list of stories which you can buy at the same store where you got this book.

Don't throw away the Wrapper

Use it as a handy catalog of the books you want some day to have. But in case you do mislay it, write to the Publishers for a complete catalog.

THE TOM SWIFT SERIES
By VICTOR APPLETON

**Uniform Style of Binding.   Individual Colored Wrappers.
Every Volume Complete in Itself.**

Every boy possesses some form of inventive genius. Tom Swift is a bright, ingenious boy and his inventions and adventures make the most interesting kind of reading.

TOM SWIFT AND HIS MOTOR CYCLE
TOM SWIFT AND HIS MOTOR BOAT
TOM SWIFT AND HIS AIRSHIP
TOM SWIFT AND HIS SUBMARINE BOAT
TOM SWIFT AND HIS ELECTRIC RUNABOUT
TOM SWIFT AND HIS WIRELESS MESSAGE
TOM SWIFT AMONG THE DIAMOND MAKERS
TOM SWIFT IN THE CAVES OF ICE
TOM SWIFT AND HIS SKY RACER
TOM SWIFT AND HIS ELECTRIC RIFLE
TOM SWIFT IN THE CITY OF GOLD
TOM SWIFT AND HIS AIR GLIDER
TOM SWIFT IN CAPTIVITY
TOM SWIFT AND HIS WIZARD CAMERA
TOM SWIFT AND HIS GREAT SEARCHLIGHT
TOM SWIFT AND HIS GIANT CANNON
TOM SWIFT AND HIS PHOTO TELEPHONE
TOM SWIFT AND HIS AERIAL WARSHIP
TOM SWIFT AND HIS BIG TUNNEL
TOM SWIFT IN THE LAND OF WONDERS
TOM SWIFT AND HIS WAR TANK
TOM SWIFT AND HIS AIR SCOUT
TOM SWIFT AND HIS UNDERSEA SEARCH
TOM SWIFT AMONG THE FIRE FIGHTERS
TOM SWIFT AND HIS ELECTRIC LOCOMOTIVE
TOM SWIFT AND HIS FLYING BOAT
TOM SWIFT AND HIS GREAT OIL GUSHER
TOM SWIFT AND HIS CHEST OF SECRETS
TOM SWIFT AND HIS AIRLINE EXPRESS

GROSSET & DUNLAP,   PUBLISHERS,   NEW YORK

THE DON STURDY SERIES
By VICTOR APPLETON

Individual Colored Wrappers and Text Illustrations by
WALTER S. ROGERS
Every Volume Complete in Itself

In company with his uncles, one a mighty hunter and the other a noted scientist, Don Sturdy travels far and wide, gaining much useful knowledge and meeting many thrilling adventures.

DON STURDY ON THE DESERT OF MYS-
Or, Autoing in the Land of the Caravans.   TERY;
An engrossing tale of the Sahara Desert, of encounters with wild animals and crafty Arabs.

DON STURDY WITH THE BIG SNAKE
Or, Lost in the Jungles of the Amazon.   HUNTERS;
Don's uncle, the hunter, took an order for some of the biggest snakes to be found in South America—to be delivered alive! The filling of that order brought keen excitement to the boy.

DON STURDY IN THE TOMBS OF GOLD;
Or, The Old Egyptian's Great Secret.
A fascinating tale of exploration and adventure in the Valley of Kings in Egypt. Once the whole party became lost in the maze of cavelike tombs far underground.

DON STURDY ACROSS THE NORTH POLE;
Or, Cast Away in the Land of Ice.
Don and his uncles joined an expedition bound by air across the north pole. A great polar blizzard nearly wrecks the airship.

DON STURDY IN THE LAND OF VOLCANOES;
Or, The Trail of the Ten Thousand Smokes.
An absorbing tale of adventures among the volcanoes of Alaska in a territory but recently explored. A story that will make Don dearer to his readers than ever.

GROSSET & DUNLAP,   PUBLISHERS,   NEW YORK

THE RAILROAD SERIES

By ALLEN CHAPMAN
Author of the "Radio Boys," Etc.

Uniform Style of Binding. Illustrated.
Every Volume Complete in Itself.

In this line of books there is revealed the whole workings of a great American railroad system. There are adventures in abundance—railroad wrecks, dashes through forest fires, the pursuit of a "wildcat" locomotive, the disappearance of a pay car with a large sum of money on board—but there is much more than this—the intense rivalry among railroads and railroad men, the working out of running schedules, the getting through "on time" in spite of all obstacles, and the manipulation of railroad securities by evil men who wish to rule or ruin.

RALPH OF THE ROUND HOUSE;
Or, Bound to Become a Railroad Man.

RALPH IN THE SWITCH TOWER;
Or, Clearing the Track.

RALPH ON THE ENGINE;
Or, The Young Fireman of the Limited Mail.

RALPH ON THE OVERLAND EXPRESS;
Or, The Trials and Triumphs of a Young Engineer.

RALPH, THE TRAIN DISPATCHER;
Or, the Mystery of the Pay Car.

RALPH ON THE ARMY TRAIN;
Or, The Young Railroader's Most Daring Exploit.

RALPH ON THE MIDNIGHT FLYER;
Or, The Wreck at Shadow Valley.

RALPH AND THE MISSING MAIL POUCH;
Or, The Stolen Government Bonds.

GROSSET & DUNLAP, Publishers, NEW YORK

THE RIDDLE CLUB BOOKS
By ALICE DALE HARDY

**Individual Colored Wrappers. Attractively Illustrated.
Every Volume Complete in Itself.**

Here is as ingenious a series of books for little folks as
has ever appeared since " Alice in Wonderland." The idea
of the Riddle books is a little group of children—three girls
and three boys decide to form a riddle club. Each book is
full of the adventures and doings of these six youngsters,
but as an added attraction each book is filled with a lot of
the best riddles you ever heard.

THE RIDDLE CLUB AT HOME

An absorbing tale that all boys and girls will enjoy reading.
How the members of the club fixed up a clubroom in the Larue
barn, and how they, later on, helped solve a most mysterious
happening, and how one of the members won a valuable prize,
is told in a manner to please every young reader.

THE RIDDLE CLUB IN CAMP

The club members went into camp on the edge of a beautiful
lake. Here they had rousing good times swimming, boating
and around the campfire. They fell in with a mysterious old man
known as The Hermit of Triangle Island. Nobody knew his
real name or where he came from until the propounding of a
riddle solved these perplexing questions.

THE RIDDLE CLUB THROUGH THE
HOLIDAYS

This volume takes in a great number of winter sports, including skating and sledding and the building of a huge snowman.
It also gives the particulars of how the club treasurer lost the
dues entrusted to his care and what the melting of the great
snowman revealed.

THE RIDDLE CLUB AT SUNRISE BEACH

This volume tells how the club journeyed to the seashore and
how they not only kept up their riddles but likewise had good
times on the sand and on the water. Once they got lost in a fog
and are marooned on an island. Here they made a discovery
that greatly pleased the folks at home.

GROSSET & DUNLAP, Publishers, NEW YORK